FML:

FUCK MY LIFE

A novel by *Mimi Ray*

FML: FUCK MY LIFE
A novel by *Mimi Ray*

FML: FUCK MY LIFE

This is a work of fiction. All of the characters, organizations, and events portrayed in this novel are either products of the author's imagination or are used fictitiously. Any resemblance to actual persons, living or dead is purely coincidental.

FML: FUCK MY LIFE
A novel by *Mimi Ray*

Acknowledgements

I'm not a super religious person but I was raised to believe in GOD. Life handed me challenges and somehow I overcame them. I prayed and He answered!! Thank you, Higher Being for keeping me sane.

I never would have made it without the love and support from my mom Karen A., stepdad Milton J., grandma Mattie C., goddaughter Jasmine Damira B., children, DaGod and Goddess, their dads, Leonard & Taeron, their "fairy" godmother Karen K. and the best King that a Queen could ask for, my

FML: FUCK MY LIFE
A novel by *Mimi Ray*

husband Shawn Ray. Without y'all, there's no me!!

To my brothers, Brandon T. and Chris T., hold ya heads up! RIP Purnell Jennings Jr aka Worly.. Never to be forgotten.

Special thanks to my best friends of over two decades (telling our ages) lol... Shawntay B., Nicole S., Michele W., Shanta W., Annette P., Davon B., Dante W. and Nneka C.!! 25 years and going!!

To my chicks for life...ride or die! I love y'all for always having my back even when I'm being bipolar! Jewel T.,Sharon S., Kalema N., Shantel H., Porche R., and my male BFF Antoine S.!!

To my very best friend in a class of her own, Vernetta D. Lomax (sometimes Green) I love you, you crazy bitch!!! FML! Lmao, no one understands us,   but   we   do!

FML: FUCK MY LIFE
A novel by *Mimi Ray*

Shout out to my test readers!! Sharita B., Shawnta E. ,Keisha H. and Josephine J.... Y'all let me bug y'all when everyone else dropped out!! I appreciate the   feedback!!

To my VSpot fam & my Edenwald ladies... Thanks for allowing me to nag y'all day in and day out!! You   all   are   thee   best!!

Thank you Roni J. and Ashley M. for encouraging me to write it out and publish it! And last but not least, thanks to my publishing company, Blaque Diamond Publications and all the staff, for welcoming me with open arms! #Team Bank Roll Squad! Mimi Ray, here to stay!! Baltimore Stand Up!

FML:

FUCK MY LIFE

A novel by *Mimi Ray*

FML: FUCK MY LIFE
A novel by *Mimi Ray*

FML: FUCK MY LIFE
A novel by *Mimi Ray*

Prologue

The smell of his alcoholic breath made my stomach flip once again. I was becoming intolerant to his raggedy appearance. It seemed to be a weekly ritual for my grandmothers' homely husband to come into my bedroom on Sundays to explore my gradually changing body, while my drunken grandmother slept in their room, only two doors away. He made us call him grandpa, although he wasn't our mothers' father. We, my brothers and I, had only been living with them for three months and already he had fucked me over ten times. The first few times my pussy bled horribly for a couple of days then gradually the soreness and bleeding faded away. After some time, it became easier physically but harder mentally. My body became accustomed to this continued abuse but mentally it was beginning to take its toll. I didn't really understand what "fucking" was but the more he said "am I fucking you good? Do you like to be fucked? Who fucks you better?" I began to understand what "fucking" was. He would say, "This pussy is so innocent, this pussy is so pure, I love this saintly pussy", so frequently that I believed pussy was a valuable thing. He seemed to like it so much that he even brought his brother to my room to get some "angelic holy pussy", as he called it.

FML: FUCK MY LIFE
A novel by *Mimi Ray*

Fucking the brother was worse than fucking him. Besides the fact that he was even older, walking with a cane and noticeably handicapped, he spit when he talked and his mouth odor was horrendous. He had a shiny bald head with big gray eyebrows and an oversized gray mustache with sideburns. His clothes were raggedy with dried fish blood smeared on his plaid shirt and he smelled like he hadn't showered once in his life. These fishermen were repulsive!

He reacted as if he hit the lottery jackpot. He was excited and eager and rubbed his hands together vigorously as if he was preparing for gold to drop from the sky. Once he managed to position himself at the end of my small bed, I just opened my legs, hoping it would be over quickly. He complimented me on how pretty my pussy was after using a flashlight and examining it for a few seconds. That was a first and had me feeling weird. But then he said, "This will be the prettiest pussy I've eaten thus far," and the weird feeling lifted and I was more afraid that he was about to eat me with a knife and fork than I was of him fucking me! I had never heard of "eating pussy!" I was scared shitless! He eagerly put his mouth on my pussy and licked it up like a cat licks milk. I was sure I was about to die! In between slopping on my pussy he would say, "mmm" and "so sweet." When I realized it wasn't painful I became less afraid but nevertheless, wished he would hurry the fuck up. He was preparing to finger pop me, which I could tell because I saw him lick his fingers the same way grandpa did in the past. Then, he inserted one finger and gradually entered a second all the while I was squirming trying to stop the uncomfortable burning his probing fingers created. His dick was huge and he spent more time forcing it in than he spent inside of it. He murmured how tight and wet and warm my pussy was and when he began to climax his eyes rolled into the back of his head and he shuttered a little as a slither of drool seeped from the corner of his mouth and hung midair. As cruel as it was to be molested by this animal, I couldn't help think that I'd rather die, than to have that drool drip into my mouth or anywhere on my face. I pursed my lips together so hard and prayed, "Please God don't let it fall, please God don't let it fall," With my hands clutched so tight that my finger nails dug into my palms and produced a sticky sweaty coat. I held my breath for as long as that saliva dangled midair and when it finally landed on my stained pink nightgown I drew a refreshing breath of relief. Thank God it was only one time with the brother but grandpa made sure he got his turns religiously.

I knew it was immoral, even though no one told me, but the way he would whisper, "Bitch if you ever tell a soul I'll gut you like a fish" made me aware that it should be kept a secret. One time I

FML: FUCK MY LIFE
A novel by *Mimi Ray*

pretended to be asleep so he would hurry and get it over with and even while I fake snored, he still did his deed. He disgusted me from my intestines to my stomach, and once I vomited before he was done. He completely grossed me out, from his nappy matted gray hair, his ashy dry skin to his big dirty rough hands and worst of all, the funky fishiness of his body, from all those hours he spent at the pier.

Once, when I had finally gotten the courage to tell my grandmother, I walked into their foul smelling, perverse bedroom, to confess what had been happening, but low and behold, he was fucking her too. I swiftly left the room after seeing my grandmothers' legs in the air. I started not to care if he killed me, but when he threatened to kill my little brothers, I knew I better shut the fuck up and give him his gift of pussy.

FML: FUCK MY LIFE
A novel by *Mimi Ray*

1989

So what I was thirteen years old, I had already deemed myself as being "Grown." If you had a crack head mother, an alcoholic grandmother, a child molesting grandfather and a dope fiend father that you never knew, you would grow up fast too. It had been almost a year since I started taking over. At first our mother used to stay the night with us, even if she didn't get in until the wee hours of the morning. Slowly we started seeing her less. She would come once a week, bringing a bag of groceries with not nearly enough food for us to eat but we were happy as hell to have food. Before you knew it, she just didn't come at all. The house was section 8 and I never really knew how the rent worked but I recalled that she said it was free as long as the gas and electric were on. We all went to school every day, at first, then some kids started asking questions, so I pretended that our mother was sick and that's when I stopped going altogether and said I was staying at home to take care of her. Naturally, being as though I was the oldest of us four, I had to quit school to look out for my little brothers. I wasn't sure if I could actually call what I was doing, "looking out," but we managed to survive. Most days we would take turns going on the corner begging for change until we had enough money to get dinner, the usual, penny cookies. With twenty five cents each we could get fifteen cookies a piece. I never let the boys miss school because I knew they could get free breakfast and lunch but on the weekends, when school was closed, it was tough to come up with three meals a day. We learned how to make one pack of Ramen noodles stretch to feed four hungry stomachs. Sometimes, if we were lucky enough we would stretch it with a boiled egg and one hot dog. We learned that syrup sandwiches could last a few days if we used one slice of bread each and drank a large cup of water. We were okay surviving in that manner until some nosey fucking neighbors discovered we had illegal gas and electric and called the police. The night the police came, we hid under the bed and pretended no one was home. We could hear the elderly old lady from next door snitching, saying she had seen us looking out of the window. The police continued to knock and threatened to come inside and get us, causing Chink to cry out hysterically. Since my attempts to calm him failed, I sent Worm to open the front door. Once inside, the officers looked us over and their faces actually showed concern. It was roaches crawling all over, looking for food, because, I believe, they were hungry too. The older looking female officer questioned Booker and I answered for him. I was the head of the household and I didn't allow anyone too close to my brothers. If our

FML: FUCK MY LIFE
A novel by *Mimi Ray*

mother didn't care about her own flesh and blood, I
surely didn't trust that any ole' stranger in a uniform
cared. I lied with a straight face and said our
mother was working late and she had bombed the
house with bug foggers, to try to explain the roach
infestation. The truth was, our mother never held a
job in her life and the roaches were no big deal
because we had gotten used to them being around.
But I was smart enough not to tell them that and I
damn sure wasn't about to say that she left with a
man and we hadn't seen her in months. I just kept
answering their questions, swiftly coming up with
lie after lie until a lady showed up from Child
Protective Services.

The lady, short and chubby with an afro,
wearing makeup too dark for her skin, was
extremely polite. But still, when she asked
questions, I lied to her too. All I wanted them to do
was get the fuck out of my house and once Chink
started crying again, that's exactly what I yelled,
"Leave us the hell alone and get the fuck out of my
house!!" They all looked surprised that a young girl
like me had a dynamic voice like that, and wasn't
backing down from four adults. I was making a
scene, cussing and fussing and began throwing half
empty cups, hardback books, steel toe boots and
anything else I could find towards the officers.

In the midst of my courageous attempt to
regain control of my household, they were escorting

my brothers outside. I was kicking and screaming as the lady officer tried to subdue me and the next thing you know, all of us was in the back seat of a squad car all bunched up and only I had handcuffs on my wrists. I didn't know their intentions but I kept telling my brothers that everything would be ok and in my heart I believed it would. We spent what seemed to be forever in the back of the squad car until it finally sped off, sirens wailing and all. I just knew I was being taken to jail, I didn't even feel scared for myself but I was scared for my brothers. I didn't know where they would take them if they took me to jail. However, I was looking out the window, and about twenty minutes later, I recognized the busy street filled with tall row houses and I was not at all happy that we were pulling up at our grandmothers' old broken down house, which was where our mother was raised.

The big three story row home was located in a crime ridden drug infested neighborhood in East Baltimore. It had five huge bedrooms and two bathrooms with two sets of stairs to connect three levels. The furnishings were old, the paint was peeling from the dingy walls and it was so many mice running around that the two tabby cats didn't attempt to chase them. No one cleaned up there and it smelled like musty piss. Two of the bedrooms, located on the third floor, were filled with junk, boxes, old furniture and bags of unlabeled mystery items. The largest bedroom in the front, on the second floor was grandmas' room which left the two smaller rooms on the second floor to be shared between my brothers and I. Automatically grandma assigned the back room to me so the boys would be closest to her room, since she said she, "Wanted to keep an eye on them."

We could tell that we weren't welcomed there, not because we were kids, but we were Pam's kids. Pam was the black sheep of the family. She had four kids by age twenty one and she had been using drugs since her first pregnancy, with me, at fifteen. No one felt obligated to help Pam because she had stolen from her family, lied continuously, and did a lot of manipulative dirt to keep her habit fed.

It had been about four months of living in hell, as I called it and I was growing tired of begging for loose change. Grandma had gotten a lock on her refrigerator and freezer so I was hoping to discover a way to keep my brothers and I fed. While begging for change one day, I heard this young guy wearing gold chains and stylish clothes say to a half-naked lady in a short mini skirt, "Crawler said, how much for some pussy?" and when she replied, "Tell Crawler, $100," My ears stood up.

It was time to really look out for my brothers and the easiest way to do this was "using what I got to get what I want." Developing into a shapely big booty bitch, I had all the neighborhood guys' eyes on me. But I quickly decided, the only way their hands would get on me was with cash; long cash. I gave up enough free pussy to my sinful ill-behaved grandfather and his filthy brother. Never once did those old bastards give me a dollar after feeling me up, finger popping my tight young pussy, rubbing their dirty gray haired dicks on my growing round ass and taking my innocence; my virginity. Just thinking back, gave me chills. One day they will pay with their souls. But right now, these dumb ass East Baltimore niggas will pay with their pockets; starting with Crawler.

FML: FUCK MY LIFE
A novel by *Mimi Ray*

Easy Target

"Shut the fuck up you bald headed slut!!" he yelled as he kicked a neighborhood crack head that was kneeled over. I couldn't see her face but I could easily tell she was a user. She had to be about 100 pounds, soaking wet. "Where the fuck did you find this bag?" He asked. She was trying to reply but every time she opened her mouth he kicked her again. I was watching from the broken kitchen window of my grandparents' house and although I had seen him around the neighborhood beating on people before, this time he seemed super furious. I was wondering what bag she found and what was in it that had him pissed off. He yelled a few more curse words and kicked her a few more times before she went limp. He dragged her into an abandoned house and was now out of my view.

Crawler was an ugly little motherfucker. When you looked at his face it could easily remind you of the Gremlin leader, Spike. He was short, about 5'3 and so dark, even his eyeballs were brown stained. Now chocolate men were my favorite but Crawler didn't have a sexy bone in his body. He had crooked discolored teeth and I'm sure a few were missing. However, because he was known to be a crazy lead infected nigga, he got the upmost respect from niggas and bitches. He stayed fresh, with the latest fashion and always looked clean. There was a saying that insinuated that ugly niggas needed to stay fresh, to distract you from their bad looks and he was a prime example of that saying. I knew he had to be slinging a long dick because he had a whole line of women and money alone couldn't get that many hoes. But right now I couldn't give a rats' ass about those hoes, I needed a couple hundred dollars for some groceries and toiletries and Crawler should be an easy target. I've caught him eyeing me before at The Corner Carryout.

I knew exactly what I was doing. As soon as I saw Crawler exiting the abandoned house, I cheerfully grabbed the bag of garbage I had put together and flirtatiously walked out the back door with just my pink and black studded bra and little black boy shorts on. The cool breeze immediately made my 36C nipples hard and I was thinking "How perfect, that even the weather was on my team!" At the same moment he reached my rat ridden backyard, I reached the trashcan. I dropped the bag, on purpose, and seductively bent over to be sure he saw my entire big curvy brown ass. Jackpot! I could hear him saying "What's up girl?" I turned and said "Not a thing" and pranced toward my back door as he said to my back, "Come here, let me holla at you." I turned to face him and said, "Hurry up because it's cold out here, what you want?" "Just a minute of your time", he replied slyly. I'm thinking, "This will be easier than I thought, maybe I can charge by the minute."

I'd been getting hit off a nice amount by Crawler and a couple other neighborhood hustlers but I still believed in budgeting my money. I pretty much had managed to line up at least three guys a week and word that I was "Getting down," traveled fast. Evidently I was becoming a hot topic because guys were looking for me left and right. I was adamant on making as much money as I could; while I could, so I formulated a waiting list. Basically you had to wait your turn but if your price was right, someone else got bumped. I was saving money, purchasing only necessities and formulating a plan to move my brothers and me out of the "Hell house."

"Damn these prices are getting higher and higher!" I said to myself, as I put food in the raggedy shopping cart at dirty ass Big B Supermarket. I was diplomatic about maintaining my money and soon discovered that stealing was a great way to budget. Lucky for me, I wore my big gray coat, unlucky for the black business owners. I filled my coat with three packs of chicken wings and four packs of sliced deli lunch meat. "The rest of this crap I can pay for. I don't even eat this shit but the boys like it and I'll do anything for them," I was mumbling as I thought about where the grocery money had come from. Shit, fucking Crawler was easy for $200 a session. His dick wasn't too big and I even managed to cum. A cum is always a bonus when fucking for cash.

One day last week when we hooked up I decided to do a little extra for a little extra. We went to his homeboy house over on Register Street. I tossed my usual toiletries in my hoe bag and threw in a bottle of Chocolate Syrup. Crawler had the stamina of a horse and he could go for at least an hour before the first nut. Sometimes that was a plus; sometimes not, depending on how many other guys I fucked during the week. On that particular night I had a mission to get him to bust off in thirty minutes or less. I allowed him to take the lead as usual. He would spread my pussy lips wide with both hands and slurp all my juices not missing a drop. He did this thing with his tongue that kept my clit erect for minutes. Most times I'd cum and fall weak but that night I held back. I reached over and pulled the chocolate syrup out of my bag, drizzled small amounts onto my nipples and pussy and had him start all over. He was so turned on I could tell my plan was heading in the right direction. After I couldn't take the pleasure any longer I pushed him up off of me and climbed onto his smooth thick dick. Up and down I went as I used all of my energy to keep the same rhythm for my mission was to "Get that cum." The way my hips gyrated and pussy gripped his dick, I could feel his nut was building up. I sat up straight and took all the dick deep inside me and after three more minutes of riding him like a bull, he grabbed my ass, pulled me closer and I could feel the vibration as his heavy load of cum filled me up. I smiled at the flashback. Damn I was good.

FML: FUCK MY LIFE
A novel by *Mimi Ray*

Unwanted

I vomited three more times since leaving the clinic last night. That dumb ass doctor said I should feel fine but he obviously lied. My first abortion wasn't easy as I had heard that they were. After sitting in a waiting room with about twenty other women, for three and a half hours they finally took me to the back. Everything was set up like an operating room with a large machine beside the small cot that I was told to lie on. A handsome white doctor, poked, prodded and prepped me while his assistant injected me with medication. All I know is I became drowsy and when I woke up he told me I was no longer pregnant.

The nurse gave me some nasty ass unsalted crackers to eat and bland sugar free juice to drink then I started vomiting. What they told me would be a four hour procedure turned into an all damn day event. That fucking procedure was exhausting, then again it could have been the untreated gonorrhea that damn near caused me to have Pelvic Inflammatory Disease. I didn't know what the fuck that was and after reading the pamphlet, the nurse had given me, I was thankful it could be prevented with treatment. I had been ignoring the stomach pain for a couple of months since I had no time to be sick; I was busy stacking cash. Shit I thought it was all related to my missed periods and in my opinion, missed periods were a godsend; that meant I could fuck every day if I wanted. If my mother wasn't so busy chasing crack, she could have explained how periods work years ago but the nurse had given me a pamphlet on menstrual cycles too. One thing I was certain of, as soon as the doctor said, I'm not only pregnant, but I'm carrying a Sexually Transmitted Disease, I knew the only one I contracted it from had to be Crawler; he was the only one I let fuck me raw. Abortion was my only option cause I'll be damned if I was gonna birth a gremlin baby! I mean it's been two years of fucking and he keeps my pockets well filled but no damn disease and ugly baby is worth this. Just wait until I see him tonight, I'm gonna make him pay. This time, a Monument Mall shopping spree won't be enough. Besides, Worm, my oldest little brother is turning fourteen next Friday and I want to give him a big birthday party.

FML: FUCK MY LIFE
A novel by *Mimi Ray*

The Brothers

Worm has really blossomed to a fine young man. His mocha skin and deep wavy hair always had gotten him attention. He's about 5'7 now and gaining weight. I see the little bitties eyeing him and he's probably not a virgin anymore but I won't ask. Worm has a lot of hatred in his heart. He can't remember when our mom was a good mom. I think she started with hardcore drugs when he was about five so all he recalls is everything bad; her not coming home, her not feeding him and her not caring. His father died of AIDS a few years ago. Rumor had it that he caught it in prison fucking with faggots. I never asked; because I never cared. All his father ever gave me was my brother. I never knew the man.

Booker my middle younger brother was fine as he can be at twelve years old. I swear, his father had good genes; smooth chocolate skin and beautiful white teeth, he was sure to catch a few women and make some pretty babies. Only problem with him; his attitude. He felt as though the world owed him something. I guess all he can remember is two crack head parents abandoning him. Once when I was in sixth grade, I came home and found him pissy wet and shitty on the floor with neither our mother nor his father around. My mother was just a worthless piece of shit. Four kids with three different fathers, as she tells it. I believe its four different fathers myself. There's no other way to explain my youngest brother, Chink. He's nine months younger than Booker and he doesn't look like any of us. He was light skin with chinky eyes and nappy headed with a big nose. But we loved him. He was born a preemie crack baby so we all automatically felt we needed to protect him. He's just as crazy as they come, and I'm sure he has lead poisoning.

Booker and Chink were the only two with the same last name but they were as different as apples and oranges. Booker would stay to himself for the most part unless he was with Worm. I wasn't sure which one of the two was more aggressive. Once it was a neighborhood fight and while Booker was walking past, he got punched. He ran into the house to get Worm and all hell broke loose. Worm ran and grabbed a big metal bat and headed out the door without a skipping a beat. He wasted no time asking questions. He swung the bat into the crowd, hitting anyone in his path. A few people scattered. Others were screaming and a few got hit. Booker must have caught a thrill from watching Worm because he ran back inside and before I could stop him, he was out the door with a damn machete! I was sure their asses were going to jail! But people just ran and cleared the area as I yelled from the door for them to bring their asses in the house.

FML: FUCK MY LIFE
A novel by *Mimi Ray*

For weeks after that fight, they were known as the "crazy brothers". No one thought to fuck with them and because Chink always looked like he was going to snap at any moment, everyone thought he was crazy too. A lot of the neighborhood people didn't know me. I didn't play outside, cause remember, I was busy being grown and playing mom. And for all the times I went into the stores alone, no one ever asked me why I wasn't in school or where were my parents. For people to be so nosey, they sure didn't worry themselves with a "Grown ass little girl," as I would hear them whisper.

FML: FUCK MY LIFE
A novel by *Mimi Ray*

A Blur

I rolled over and opened my eyes, adjusting my vision to adapt to the darkness. I could finally make out that I was laying down facing a wall and I stared at the unfamiliar colorful wallpaper, while trying to figure out where the fuck I was. I vaguely remembered last night. Was it night? It's pretty dark in the room so I'm really unsure. The sour stench of garbage and alcohol burned my nose and made me feel nauseas. I decided to get up off the dirty mattress I was laying on, while being mad at myself for even laying on it. "Where the hell am I, and why can't I remember?" I thought to myself. I stepped on some trash and kicked a beer bottle while walking towards a broken window. Looking out I can't tell if its 6pm or 6am. The orange tinged sky tells me it could be either. The old gray building across the street doesn't look familiar and the two old cars parked below look abandoned. "Think Tasha, think," I say to myself. Everything really was a blur. I guess I better get out of here, wherever I am.

After walking and feeling my way around down a long narrow hallway, I find my way to the stairwell, and I see what looks like blood on the floor and the walls. Then all of a sudden I feel a sharp pain on the right side of my head, I touch it and feel a knot on my temple. "What the hell?" I say out loud but to myself. Nothing is making sense; but at least I'm not bleeding. I make it to the bottom of the stairs and see a figure lying near the doorway. I can't tell if it's a person or a dog but whatever it is, it looked lifeless. I stand there puzzled and feel fright overcome me. It's a person! A dead damn person! I see the brains splattered on the door and blood by the head. It's a boy or a short man. I had to get a closer look. I slowly walk over and I can immediately tell who it is; Crawler. Who shot Crawler? Did they hit me? Did he hit me? I'm praying I can remember. But right now I better get the fuck out of there. So that's what I do. I open the door and haul ass; hoping no one sees me.

I finally reached home, after walking about three miles. The sun began coming up, which meant I was out all night. When I got inside I looked at the clock, "6:44 a.m." and the house was quiet. I walked upstairs and saw the door to the middle bedroom was open, I peeped in; the boys were all asleep. My grandmother's door was closed and I heard water running in the bathroom. I figured it must have been grandpa so I tiptoed quietly and went into my room. I laid in my bed, under the covers, fully clothed. I smelled like weed. "I don't smoke!" I thought to myself, panicking. I began wrecking my brain trying to recall what had happened. I remember Crawler asking me to smoke something and I told him that I didn't smoke. We were sitting in an old house, downstairs on an old beat up couch and I recall telling him that the house stunk and I didn't want to be there. I was going to tell him about the STD and the abortion but he kept talking about some nigga he was trying to catch up with that owed him money. He was smoking a joint, because I remember watching him roll it up with Top Paper, licking it and then putting it up to my nose. I think smelling it kinda turned me on. He asked me about taking a shotgun, and I asked what that was; he explained it then showed me. I remember trying it and not feeling anything. He asked me did I hear something and I didn't. Then he told me that he would be right back but I don't remember where he went. "Why can't I remember much?" I thought to myself, still wrecking my brain.

FML: FUCK MY LIFE
A novel by *Mimi Ray*

Mr. Gold Teeth

The neighborhood news traveled about Crawler being killed, and the eyewitness news reported "No leads or suspects". I wasn't sure how to feel about that. That meant anyone could have known I was there with Crawler and that same anyone could have hit me in the head. I knew I had to stay focused and keep my eyes open. Crawler's funeral was the morning of Worm's 14th birthday. It was fairly nice weather and I planned to celebrate with my brother that night. I was determined that no funeral would keep me down. I really didn't feel sad. I felt confused and pissed cause it hit me that Crawler was my main money supplier. Fuck it! I wasn't blessed with these perky breasts and this phat bubble butt just to mourn over an ugly nigga!

With that thought in mind I strutted to the corner, caught a hack and arrived at Crawler's funeral with my eyes wide open for my next money man. I knew the hustlers would show up because Crawler, as everyone knew, was a known hustler.

It took me all of twenty minutes to find my next target. From the looks of things, he was flashy. Not the type I usually go for, because I'm not for all the attention. But for some reason my eyes kept roaming to his direction. He was brown skin, about 5'9 with a medium build. Sporting a regular hair cut with waves, a nice beard and it appeared he had gold teeth, my least favorite. Shit I'm not gonna have time to discriminate right now, my mission is cash, and tonight I need some for Worms' birthday celebration.

As soon as I saw Mr. Gold Teeth walking towards the exit, I quickly walked towards him with my head down, bumping into him gently. "I'm so sorry, excuse me," I said with meaning in my eyes. "No problem, little lady," He replied. I had to think quick, so I said, "I'm going to look mighty foolish standing at the bus stop with these funeral clothes on, if my buddy Crawler was alive, he would give me a ride," fake tears started falling from my eyes. "Damn I'm good!" I thought to myself. I hadn't even worked on the fake tears but they were a hit, because his next words were, "I'll take you where you got to go, he was my buddy too," And that was music to my ears. He walked me to his car, which was average; a red Maxima with nice tint. He introduced himself as "Scooter"; not the name I imagined but it will do. All the while I was thinking, I really hope those gold teeth are fronts.

I can't believe I sat in Scooter's car and talked for two hours. He believed me when I told him I was seventeen, as most guys do after seeing my well developed body. We clicked quickly and even though he was twenty- five; the oldest guy I had approached thus far, I didn't feel inferior.

FML: FUCK MY LIFE
A novel by *Mimi Ray*

That had to be the first time ever in my life finding any man that interesting, to deserve that much of my conversation. Even without plotting to get money from him, after telling him of Worm's birthday and my inability to come up with any money, he unselfishly peeled off five hundred dollar bills. I knew he was a flashy type of fella, and he was eager to impress me. He asked to see me the next day and gave me two pager numbers with code 111.

FML: FUCK MY LIFE
A novel by *Mimi Ray*

Nightmare

Once again I had awakened in a sweat from yet another nightmare. This one was different than the others. While usually it's dark and scary, this one was amazingly vivid and I could see very clear.

I was in a very well lit up hallway with doors on both side of the walls, it's very long and freezing cold. It almost reminds me of a hospitals' hallway but it's no nurses or doctors or any other people or equipment around. It was at least a quarter mile long, very narrow and the ceiling was noticeably short. No wall paper, no wooden doors or silver doorknobs. It was all gray cement with a hint of blue and that probably contributed to it being so cold. All the doors were even with the walls. You opened them by sliding your hand over a little black pad the size of your thumb to open it and it slid to the left into the wall. I see everything in a first person view, as if I'm outside of my body, watching myself. I'm holding a long black gun, I'm dressed in winter gear. A white thick leather bomber jacket and pants kinda like a soldier, marine or something. And for some reason I know that I'm underground. I walk down the narrow hall holding my rifle aimed as if I'm hunting someone or something. I check every single room. The rooms are the same as the halls plain and simple no

FML: FUCK MY LIFE
A novel by *Mimi Ray*

widows no pictures, nothing. They are very small with more cement walls. Small but large enough to fit a twin sized bed and still have like 4x6feet left of room. There is a closet in every room. On the left side of the wall. It opens just like the doors that leads into the rooms. They are also extremely small. There is a bar to hang clothes and a little rack on the floor to put shoes or something. But in every single one I find nothing, every room every closet every time I step back into the hall way I find nothing. I'm not sure what I'm looking for or why I'm even looking but I know that I have to! This goes on for a very uncomfortably long time. My panic grows as I go down the hall still checking each room starting to expect something to jump out at me. I eventually get so frantic that I open the doors and stand against the walls and peak in before actually going in. My heart beats faster like it's about to burst every time I check a room and closet. I'm starting to sweat in my gloves an army gear. I'm eventually running to each room, picking up pace. I go into this one room nothing is different. I go in. The door closes behind me. I check the closet and there is nothing. I turn and rub both eyebrows with my thumb and index finger and bring the gun back up to my shoulder. I swipe to open the door and grip my gun once more as the door proceeds to open there is a figure! As frantic and panicky as I was I pull the trigger without

FML: FUCK MY LIFE
A novel by *Mimi Ray*

hesitation. And right as I pulled that trigger I knew exactly who it was. It was Crawler. He was dressed in all black army gear as if he was in war. He had the army camouflage all over his face and neck. As he fell to the ground with three holes in his chest I look around and there are four more guys with guns but wearing the same white army gear as me. My eyes are huge and I'm extremely happy but then I'm extremely sad and mad that I killed my Crawler. My rage and regret grows within milliseconds, I feel the deep pain in my throat like I wanna cry but I don't because my tear ducts are clogged. I concentrate on crying and I feel the tears form but instead of tear drops, blood starts pouring from my eyes and I feel cleansed and start uttering strange words out loud to the guys. We all start talking in a language that I didn't recognize but we all understood each other. They disappear, vanishing into thin air and I run to the wall, reach over and swipe the thing to close the door and it closes in front of me. I'm in the room by myself once more and I lean my head against the door and let out a sigh so filled with regret, and as I closed my eyes, I wake up.

FML: FUCK MY LIFE
A novel by *Mimi Ray*

Worm's Surprise

"Listen up, listen up", said Mellie, Worm's best friend, "I just want to say thanks big sis for throwing this big bash for my boy! I'm having a good damn time even though I haven't seen Worm for the past hour! Cheers to every fucking body!!"

I'm thinking that's odd that I hadn't seen Worm for about an hour myself, but he has to be around here somewhere. He needs to show up fast because his friends are getting tore up and all this underage drinking might get some unwanted attention. I walk towards the kitchen and see my home girl Unique. She doesn't come out much since she's eight months pregnant with her second child. She's sixteen and always been big for her age so some people might not even noticed she was pregnant. "Yo Unique, you seen Worm?" I yell, noticing the music is now even louder. "I seen him about fifteen minutes ago talking to a chick out back," she yelled back. "Cool," I'm thinking, "At least he's in the area." I walked towards the living room and saw Booker and Chink talking to two chicks that look like twins. Their asses were supposed to be upstairs keeping an eye on grandma since she's drunk, once again. They knew damn well this a grown folk's party. I walked over and gave them dirty looks, not trying to embarrass them but making it known that they better clear the area. Chink saw my stern look and quickly headed towards the stairs. Booker looked at me and said, "Tasha, this is Tee and Tiff, they are Tammy sisters. I guess that makes y'all all aunties." I'm looking dumbfounded, while they're saying hello and smiling. I asked, "Who the hell is Tammy?" And they answer in unison "Worm's baby mother!" I feel sick. At the same time Worm walks through the door with a noticeably pregnant, short and cute, light brown skin chick.

FML: FUCK MY LIFE
A novel by *Mimi Ray*

Scooter

"Hey, little lady, I was hoping you paged me today," Scooter said into the telephone after I answered it. His voice was deep and masculine. I had paged him ten minutes ago and used the 111 code he gave me. He sounded excited to hear from me. "So how was your brothers' party last night, everything good?" He asked. I quickly recapped how much fun everyone had, how the crowd was larger than I anticipated and how my grandfather came home early at midnight and shut the party down. I went on, telling him of the surprising news of Worm's pregnant girlfriend. I didn't know how I felt about being an aunt, Worm was too young to be a dad. He didn't display much responsibility and I still had a few questions about that whole situation. Like where did that chick come from, how old was she, did Worm know she was pregnant before last night and why didn't she abort it? I'd ask each question soon enough.

I continued small talk with Scooter and we set a movie date for the next night, which was Sunday, the day I hated but he seemed eager to see me again. I briefly thought about what I should wear and if I should fuck him to show thanks for the five hundred dollars he gave me. My pussy tingled at the thought, which reminded me, it was a week ago that I had that abortion and I should be ready to fuck. I hadn't even thought about being horny until now. "Yea," I thought, "I will fuck Scooter tomorrow and it better be a good stress reliever."

I was really having a remarkable time while out on my date with Scooter. He was a complete gentleman. His mannerisms reminded me of the guys from some of my favorite love movies. He opened the doors for me, pulled out my seat at the table and even helped me with my coat. Even when I was overly flirtatious and making sexual advances, he seemed to brush it off and make new conversation. The man was a catch! He had intellect, style, charm and sex appeal. I felt a little insecure in his presence, and my self-doubt allowed me to question if he was out of my league. I knew I would have to do more than fuck him to keep him interested, his aura alone told me that. His extensive vocabulary intrigued me to want to learn more about him. He stood out from other street guys, and I was speculating that he had been raised in the county and went to private schools. Indeed, I wanted to explore this mystery man but I needed him to want to explore me too.

FML: FUCK MY LIFE
A novel by *Mimi Ray*

Speechless

Three weeks of talking on the phone and patiently waiting to see him again, I was pleasantly surprised when Scooter showed up at my house one afternoon and asked me to go for a ride with him. I knew I had plenty of free time before Booker and Chink would be getting out of school. He told me that he had a secret hiding spot he wanted to share with me and anything secret, I damn sure was eager to know about. We didn't drive far, as soon as I got comfortable and kicked my shoes off he was parking at what looked to be a museum. After closer observation, I realized it was a museum of some sort but it looked to be closed for business. "Come on, this way", Scooter said as he was already walking toward the rear of the building, while I was admiring the architecture. I knew I probably looked like a tourist but I didn't care. I walked up quickly catching up with Scooter. "Is this place closed?" I asked and he said, "Yes" as if it wasn't a big deal. I laughed and said, "Boy we better not go in there! You gonna get us arrested," really thinking of the possibility. "Naw, come on, trust me," He said, after getting the small side door open. He did it with such ease it seemed as if he had a key. Once inside I stood there looking around in awe. It was spectacular. The walls were mirrored from the ceiling to the floor and the ceiling had what looked like a sparkling waterfall that revolved from one side of the room to the other and back. The place was immaculate. I couldn't understand why it wasn't opened for business but I was pleased to see such a display. Scooter watched me as I looked around with amazement. There were marble statues of various animals and life size crystal angel figures in each corner. I felt as if I was floating, as slowly as I followed Scooter. He didn't seem fazed at the museum; he seemed to be enjoying watching me, as I enjoyed the museum. He led me to another room that set off to the right of the main room. In the center of the room, planted atop a mirrored floor was a large statue of a golden elephant. It was so shiny that I could see my reflection in it and I figured someone must come in frequently to dust. There were several smaller golden elephant statues in the room, posed in different positions. I never described elephants as being beautiful, but the statues were just that. We left "The elephant room" and walked directly across the parquet wooded floor to another room. Once inside, I immediately knew it was "The jungle room". It was decorated like a safari with exotic flowers and a small waterfall in the corner. This was the only room with a big plush carpet, so fluffy, I felt obliged to take my shoes off. Scooter was sitting directly in the middle of the carpet and he looked so peaceful. I was just about to ask him, if he did a lot of thinking in that room, then he said, "I come here to ease my mind," in a soft tone. I walked over and sat next to him, and gently rubbed his back. After a few minutes of quiet between us, he turned to me and kissed my forehead. He was such a gentleman. I figured that was the end of our museum visit, so I adjusted myself prepared to depart.

"I was thinking how nice it's been since you came into my life," he said, he grasped both my wrists with his hands and pulled me towards him. I went willingly and found myself cradled against his chest as I said "You're so completely unlike any guy I've met before." He had not released his gentle hold on my wrists until he had guided them comfortably to hold him around his waist. When he did let go, he again gently caressed me with his fingertips.

I drew in a breath and wondered would it be my last. I thought I could die right there and now in his warm embrace, as he began to gently caress my back and neck. "Scooter ..." I started tentatively, but the words just escaped me. "Yea Tasha?" He murmured, his lips against my forehead, his warm breath making my head swim. "Scooter, I want --" I again choked on the words. He made me feel so shy. He placed several tiny kisses on my forehead; then spoke again. "You want what?" He asked; then as he continued to gently kiss my forehead, ears and cheeks he whispered softly against my skin. "You want me to kiss you some more? Like this, or this, or perhaps this?" He laughed, but it was a soft laugh. His lips nuzzled against my ear, he spoke again. "May I tell you what I want?" He asked. "Yes!" My whole body now tingled with the intimacy of every contact between us. I longed to tell him how much I wanted him right now but speech was near Impossible. Again his voice softly caressed my senses, "I want to make love to you. I want to know every part of you inside and out. I want to make you feel something so strong that you'll never want for another. I want you to cry out my name and I want you to know that I will cherish you. Do you want me to do those things to you?" His lips were still brushing my cheek and ear as he spoke these words, my body burned with the heat of desire. "I want you," I whispered, "Make love to me, Scooter." I had never said those words before. Maybe it was the tranquil environment; whatever it was, it just seemed that those were the words I should say. His mouth met mine, kissing me softly, finally. And I parted my lips and welcomed him. What happened next, on the plush carpet, the sex we shared as if we were deeply in love, is too remarkable for words.

FML: FUCK MY LIFE
A novel by *Mimi Ray*

1992

Things had been going well for Scooter and me for a few months now. I really liked being with him. Not just because he threw money and slung the dick well but he was showing me that he had good heart with good intentions. He was romantic and spontaneous and he treated me as a woman. He was allowing Booker, Chink and I to stay at his two bedroom apartment and patiently spent countless hours showing me how to study for my GED on his computer. According to the pre-tests, I would be ready to sit down for the exam in three to four months. Just in time for my sixteenth birthday. He catered to me in a way no man had ever attempted to and made me feel special in a way no man had done before. He encouraged me to get my learners' permit and after weeks of nerve wrecking sessions behind the wheel, he managed to teach me how to drive!

Worm moved in with Tammy and their new daughter, my niece, Kashay. She's cute as she want to be and after talking with Tammy and visiting her in the hospital, I had no doubts about that chubby little love muffin being our blood. I mentioned to Worm that I heard that he had been missing school a lot and getting drunk with Mellie frequently and he promised me that he would get back on track.

FML: FUCK MY LIFE
A novel by *Mimi Ray*

Tammy was nineteen and had a section 8 apartment. I couldn't understand what she saw in my fourteen year old little brother, but apparently he's becoming a man quicker than I had noticed. They seemed to be happy together, so I was ok with that. Plus my money was tight, and with Booker and Chink with me 24/7, I was feeling like a real mother instead of big sister. My grandparents didn't say much about us not being there and we slowly moved our clothes into Scooter's apartment, which he seemed to enjoy. I hadn't put my finger on it but he was like a guardian angel, with a big dick as a bonus.

FML: FUCK MY LIFE
A novel by *Mimi Ray*

Our Mother

"I swear I hate coming to this damn school," I thought as I walked into Booker and Chink's school to get their report cards. I must say they both had been doing well since moving into Scooter's place. Chink hadn't been eating powder or licking the walls for a few months. I thought maybe he was benefiting from our new environment better than me.

I retrieved the boys and both of their report cards, which equally made me proud. Both of them had A's and B's and Booker had one C, in Latin. That was cool to me because he probably will never need that anyway. Dumb ass Baltimore City Schools. Who needs Latin?

"Can we stop at The Corner Carryout?" asked Chink. Booker quickly chimed in saying,"Yea cause I want some Now Laters anyway." I corrected him saying, "They're called Now AND Laters" and they both looked at me like I was stupid.

We walked to The Corner Carryout and a skinny dark skin lady barely looked up but said, "Hey one of y'all got a quarter?" I recognized her voice immediately; our mom, damn she looked so bad. If she hadn't had the same voice I wouldn't have recognized her, I said "No Pam, we don't have no quarters, every quarter we get we spend it on food since our mother don't feed us!" And she looked up, looking frail and sickly, she smiled and started saying "My babies, oh my God y'all are getting so big! Mama told me y'all moved with some drug dealer. She told me Worm got a damn baby. She told me social service was going to take y'all away." I interrupted her rants with swiftness, "Excuse me, we are living fine, not with no drug dealer and social service don't do nothing for us so they won't be taking us nowhere!" As much as I wanted to curse, I guess I still had an ounce of respect for her. I grabbed both of my brothers by their arms, nearly dragging them down the street and quickly away from her before they heard too much. It was just at that moment that I recognized her as the same woman Crawler was kicking in the alley before he died. She looked like a walking zombie. How pathetic. I felt no daughterly love for the woman who birthed me.

FML: FUCK MY LIFE
A novel by *Mimi Ray*

Unreal

I was all the way turned up! Scooter surprised me with a 1990 Honda Accord for my birthday. He was thinking I was turning eighteen, when actually I was turning sixteen. One thing I noticed with Scooter is that he didn't ask a lot of questions and he seemed pretty gullible for his age. I wasn't complaining, because it was all a bonus for me. He was congratulating me for passing my GED test and getting my drivers' license and he gave me an envelope with ten big faces. I was used to getting a few hundred here and there but one thousand at once meant I was all the way in there. He even introduced me as his "Lady" whenever we went out. For the most part he kept me home, fed, fucked and took care of my brothers and me. He gave me money orders to mail the rent, gas & electric payment and cable but everything else he took care of. He never discussed his business but I knew he was moving big amounts across the city. I saw him stacking money in his safe every night when I pretended to be sleep. And I managed to learn the combination, but I had no intentions of using it. As long as I played my role, we got along fine. I started realizing that I had more than feelings for Scooter; I loved him. Wow, I guess he was my first love. Crawler didn't have this effect on me and I hadn't been fucking no other dudes since I moved in Scooter's apartment. I was daydreaming about trying something new with Scooter that night, like whipped cream and handcuffs when I heard a loud ongoing knock at the door.

Bang bang bang bang! It was definitely a knock that was out of place. First off, it was almost midnight and no one ever came by, especially uninvited. I knew I had to answer before they woke the boys. I grabbed my purple plush robe that Scooter had bought me two days ago and went to the door. Looking out the tiny peephole, I saw a young looking fat chick with braids down to her breasts and a tall thin dude wearing his hat to the back. They obviously had the wrong door, so I asked "Who are y'all looking for?" without opening the door. "Is Tasha here?" The chick yelled, with an accent in her voice. Reluctantly, I replied slowly, "Yea who wants her?" The dude said sounding agitated, "Look open up shorty, Scooter sent me. I felt uneasy, but I opened the door slightly and peeped out. That's when I noticed the girl was crying, and she blurted out in that deep accent she owned, "Scooter got shot! He's on Wolfe Street! The ambulance is there but its blood everywhere!"

The weeks following Scooter's funeral were a blur. His friends took care of everything, since I was out in a daze. Not that I knew a damn thing about planning a funeral. I was feeling depressed. I never told Scooter I loved him. He never told me any wishes for our future. I learned from his friends that both of his parents had died in a house fire with his two younger brothers. It help me conclude that was probably why he was so welcoming to Booker and Chink. I realized I hadn't known much about Scooter besides he was compassionate, kindhearted and adored by many. Apparently he had talked about me to his friends because they all seemed to know me even though I didn't know them. His friends were sincere and generous. They gave me a plaque saying "Stanley Johnson Jr. aka Scooter, loved by many; never to be forgotten" and a small gift box with $3455. I was appreciative and overwhelmed with the outpour of support and I knew with that plus the cash in Scooter's safe I should be able to handle the bills for at least five months. I also knew it was time to get a job.

FML: FUCK MY LIFE
A novel by *Mimi Ray*

Bob Big Boys

It was my third week on the job and I caught on quickly. I was hired as a waitress which included clearing tables. I really wanted to work morning shift but the only shift they had available was 4pm-12am so I had to take it. This schedule took away hours from spending time with the boys but I made arrangements with Unique to look out for them after school and in exchange, I bought food for her and her two kids.

Bob Big Boys was a popular hangout for the ballers, hustlers and chicks who was trying to get down. I had put on a little weight working there and my now size twelve jeans were filled to perfection. I don't know where I inherited this big ass, but it was definitely beneficial to getting more tips. It had been four months since Scooter was murdered. I was maintaining the bills and paying my car insurance with no problem. However, the money was dwindling down and I really didn't have any extra for luxury items. The boys were going through puberty and growing faster than I could keep up. Worm was busy with his family and had stopped going to school altogether and I heard people gossiping saying he was selling crack. Whenever I went pass Tammy's house to see Kashay, Worm wasn't around. And several times I noticed Tammy's

FML: FUCK MY LIFE
A novel by *Mimi Ray*

new jewels, clothes and shoes but once I saw the flat screen television and stereo system in her living room I assumed the rumors were true.

One evening when I was clearing my last round of tables, I noticed a fifty dollar tip, with the name "Nate" and a number written on it. I knew it was for me, as I recalled three young black dudes sitting at that booth. Each one was draped in ice and labels. None of them really stood out, and they seemed too engrossed in their conversation to notice me enough to leave such a nice tip. Nevertheless I put the bill in my bra and planned on using the number the next day. "Whoever he was, maybe he had more fifties where that one came from," I thought anxiously. I mourned for Scooter long enough and as long as I wasn't fucking in his bed, he should rest in peace. Besides a girl has needs and I needed to be touched.

FML: FUCK MY LIFE
A novel by *Mimi Ray*

The Tipper

I still hadn't mastered the art of pumping gas. I wasn't sure if it was because I hated pumping it or because I didn't know what the hell I was doing but either way, going to the gas station was always a real task. I was listening to someone's music playing while my gas pumped into the tank when I recognized the dude at the next pump. Evidently he recognized me too because as soon as I looked in his direction he walked over to me. "Hey sexy, please don't tell me you're pumping fifty dollars' worth of gas with that tip I left you, it was a hidden message on it," he slyly said. I giggled and replied,

"Actually I wrote the number down then bought the gas, and I'm gonna guess that you're Nate?" He nodded his head up and down and said "Good guess, sweetness, that's me, and you remembered my name. A bonus for you," He smiled. He had a very nice smile, with straight teeth and a nice beard. I'm starting to realize I like beards. I could see some acne on his forehead but overall he wasn't a bad looking guy. I said, "Yes and thank you, I was going to use the number to thank you, but I guess now that won't be necessary," I said with slickness. He laughed out loud and replied with, "You're welcome, but let me take you out, that way you will have something else to thank me for." I could tell he was a slick talker. I was interested in some entertainment so I gave him my number and told him to use it later, hopped in my car and drove off.

Nate wasted no time calling me. Once I got home, and retrieved the voicemails, he had already left a message saying, "Smile now, thank me later, It's Nate." His voice was deep and inviting. My girl parts tingled as I replayed the message. "Yea," I thought, "Nate just may be my next date."

FML: FUCK MY LIFE
A novel by *Mimi Ray*

Northeast Station

It was a busy Friday night at Bob Big Boys as usual. The crowd was thick and the atmosphere was energetic. All around, I seen happy customers and my coworker Zena was helping me out. My section always seemed to attract the rowdy bunch. It was near the rear of the restaurant and it seemed the niggas loved being in the back. My manager, Calvin, as fine as he wanna be, walked over and told me I had a call in his office, which was out of the ordinary so immediately I felt nervous. I picked up the phone and said, "Hello this is Tasha, who's calling?" I heard heavy breathing on the phone and then "It's me big sis, these fucking dirty cops locked me up. Come get me please! I'm at Northeast Station." It was Booker. "Where the hell is that? Why the hell are you locked up and where the fuck is Unique?" I yelled but didn't wait for an answer before I ran to grab my coat, and fled out of there. I hadn't thought to tell Zena I had to leave but my manager saw me racing and he knew it was an emergency.

After asking around for directions, I walked into Northeast Station to get Booker. I filled out some papers and waited in the lobby. Two hours later, he walked out with an older White woman with him. She introduced herself as Ms. Silver and stated that although it was Booker's first arrest, he was charged with conspiracy to distribute controlled substances and that he was going to be sent to Victor Cullen Academy For Boys until his court date. I tried to be strong, but I just started crying. How did this even happen? Why would he have drugs? Who did he get them from? When was he doing all this? I felt disappointed, angry and upset. But most importantly I felt like I failed him. If I had waited for another job, with a day shift schedule, I would have been around more. Booker didn't show any emotion. That wasn't unusual; he seemed to have a heart of stone. He simply hugged me and said, "don't cry big sis, I'll be ok". Then he turned and walked away.

I called Worm to let him know what had happened with Booker. He was questioning me asking where did Booker get drugs from? Who was I letting him hang with and why wasn't I on top of things? I was thinking that Worm was really getting to grown talking to me in that manner and acting as if it was my fault. Everything that goes wrong in this family seems to be my fucking fault. Maybe because I'm the only sane one they expect me to hold things together but shit no one holds me together. I was just as upset from talking to Worm as I was about Booker. I felt like I could bash someone's head in as the stress was building up.

FML: FUCK MY LIFE
A novel by *Mimi Ray*

The Ass Whooping

Because of Worm interrogating me, I was furious by the time I reached fat ass Unique's house. I busted in without knocking and ran straight to her dirty filthy room. There were dirty clothes all over the floor, some panties with a shit stain was beside the bed and some half eaten dried up McDonalds food on the dresser. I spotted an empty bottle of MadDog 20/20 on her nightstand and two condoms beside it. When the hell did she start living like this? I hadn't noticed. She was lying across her bed in her dingy bra and big granny panties and without a second thought I plunged on her with intent to injure. I was hitting her in her face and punching her in her head like a maniac. All the while, I'm cursing with each punch. I knocked over a lamp and the only light was moonlight coming from the window. I still didn't stop. She deserved every punch. I counted on her and she failed me. Everything happened so quick all she could do was scream and swing her arms. I called her every curse word in the book and stomped her in the stomach and chest once I tackled her to the floor. I don't remember being pulled off of her but I was told it took three people. Later I reflected on the incident and I honestly didn't know why I was fighting Unique. I was just so pissed about Booker and I had to blame someone, so since I depended on her for babysitting, she unluckily got the ass whooping. Once I started thinking, I started feeling fucked up. I killed my unborn child by Crawler. Crawler was killed. Scooter was killed. My mother was a junkie. Worm damn near forgot about us. Booker was gone to the system and Chink was all I had.

FML: FUCK MY LIFE
A novel by *Mimi Ray*

Creamy Center

I never knew I could cum so much! All this silky creamy wetness was pouring out of my pussy and he was enjoying every bit of it. The hairs on my spine stood up and I was having another orgasm. These slow deep strokes he was giving me felt like no other thrusts I had ever felt. "Damn this is the kind of dick I could settle down for," I thought, as Nate was changing position and bending me over. I swiftly reached around and grabbed his long, hard throbbing dick. That Mandingo had to be at least eleven perfect inches. I never received such a lovely piece of man meat. All this time, I thought I didn't like huge dicks. Maybe it was the way he moved, maybe it was the fact that I hadn't fucked in four months or maybe I was going through some womanly changes. Whatever it was, hot damn! I was loving it. I spread my own ass cheeks to let him know I wanted it deeper. And deeper he went. His dick felt absolutely fulfilling. I didn't want it to be over. I moaned and moaned and before two minutes passed I was cumming again. "Oooh girl you got some good ass pussy! Wet this dick up!" He exclaimed and hearing him say that, once again I was cumming. He wanted a wet dick, a wet dick he would get. He slowly rubbed his fingers against my clit while continuing to long stroke my throbbing pussy from the back. Damn that felt so good. Like a million tiny electrons crawling all over my body, so intense, so exhilarating and there I was cumming again. I lost count of the orgasms but I knew damn well he helped me reach a new record. I was sweating, my heart was racing and our rhythm matched one another's. This man could fuck! Damn he deserved a medal for this performance. He pulled his dick out and told me to turn around. I obeyed without a blink. I was face to face with that big chocolate anaconda and he pressed it against my lips. What the hell? I never sucked dick! But I opened my mouth, widely as I thought I could and was eager to try something new. It tasted sweet and familiar. My sweet pussy juice was all over it; not bad, I can do this. I opened my mouth wider and puckered my lips. I sucked it. Up and down with slight friction and producing more saliva. I was enjoying it. His dick was so big I felt my eyes watering as I tried to take it all into my mouth. He pushed his dick down my throat until I gagged, then pulled slightly back. We repeated this ritual a few times as he tried to push further and further down my throat. As I kept gagging he relented, and started with short, faster strokes, fucking my mouth. The sensations all over my body left me tingling. I was past turned on, I was turned to the highest notch on the turned on meter. I was in heaven. Damn who knew I would love sucking dick? I remember crying when Crawler told me to suck his dick and look at me now, loving it. I sucked and sucked and before you know it, little bolts of lightning were striking my skin. Shockwaves washed over me. I raised my hand and pushed Nate's dick away from my mouth as I clenched my teeth and tensed. My legs shook uncontrollably and I twitched. My toes curled, as I screamed out. "I'm cumming, I'm cumming. Fuck yessss!" He started jerking his dick and in a swift movement Nate pushed my head back with one hand and aimed his dick with the other and squirted cum all over my face. I jumped at first, then I relaxed. It pulsed into my eye and stung. Then into my mouth, which he continued to hold open. His final drippings dripped down my face, my chin, to my chest and breasts. Damn! I loved that too! I could feel cum dripping out of my pussy and I realized I had cum once again.

Nate and I didn't have a lot in common. He grew up in West Baltimore and I didn't know of one street over on the west side besides West North Avenue. He lived with his older sister in Owings Mills, a county far out in West Baltimore, and he said he was single but I had suspicions that he wasn't. Once I noticed a passion mark on his neck but I pretended I didn't see it. As long as I got my piece of the great dick, I didn't care about anything else.

FML: FUCK MY LIFE
A novel by *Mimi Ray*

Nate went to court with me on Booker's court date. It wasn't good news. The judge said with the amount of drugs Booker had intended to sell he didn't feel the community was safe with him on the street. He sentenced Booker to Victor Cullen until his eighteenth birthday. Nate consoled me as I cried and Booker simply stared, looking emotionless and accepted his sentence. I had asked Tammy to let Worm know about the court date, which she said she would, however I wasn't surprised that Worm hadn't come. Nate asked me could he pay his sister to keep an eye on Chink while he took me away for the weekend. Although I was skeptical, I knew I needed to get away. I had been working hard with only one day off in the last month and it was starting to take a toll on me. I agreed since both times I met his sister, Noel, she seemed responsible and cool. She had a fifteen year old daughter and a three year old son and I knew she didn't run the streets. Chink didn't seem to care either way; he always went with the flow. As long as he had food and snacks, you hardly heard a peep out of him.

FML: FUCK MY LIFE
A novel by *Mimi Ray*

New York City

We arrived in The Big Apple at 7am. Why Nate wanted to leave Baltimore at 4am was beyond me. I was too sleepy to enjoy the scenery but I could see people were already hustling and moving about as if it was 7pm. He booked us a room on the seventeenth floor of a luxury hotel and the view from the window was amazing. The sunrise was perfect and the sky was clear. Absolutely breathtaking. I wish I had the energy to enjoy it. Nate asked me would I like to order room service or go downstairs for breakfast and I told him I'd like to have a nap. He admitted that he was a little tired too and looked at the luxurious California king bed and winked a sexy wink. I blushed and pulled my winter white fleece sweater over my head. My perky breasts sat up attentively and my small waist was glistening as my belly piercing was revealed. I was happy that I had chosen to have it done last week. It dangled with a diamond studded butterfly. It was painless and I felt sexier. I slowly inched out of my tight stonewashed Jordache jeans and was happy that I chose to go panty-less. Nate's eyes showed that he was happy too. I climbed up on the bed and embraced the silk linen and fluffy blanket. "Damn this bed feels good!" I said out loud but not trying to sound too excited. Nate slipped in the bed next to me, grabbing my soft ass and said, "but you feel even better," and smiled. His smile was like a ray of sunshine and it turned me all the way on. I felt my horny pussy start to throb and I soon forgot just how sleepy I thought I was. We started kissing and I couldn't wait to feel that big black dick inside of my pussy again! I positioned myself on my back, too excited to get fucked but he directed me to roll over and said, "I think I want you on your knees. All fours, as a matter of fact," and slapped my ass. I was a little disappointed, doggy style was nice but it didn't usually make me cum. Nevertheless, I bent over as told. Nate began to tease my ass rubbing my asshole then he dragged his index finger across my clitoris. His motions were swift. With the ease of breath, he slipped his finger inside me. I leaned into his hand and began to move my hips to his rhythm. Nate rocked my hips with his free hand, guiding me along his waves of movement. I was more than content to let him run me. His finger fit me perfectly. With a strong thrust, he angled his hand so perfectly that he was touching my g-spot as he gave me another finger to work with. I made some kind of unintelligible noise and gave completely into my pleasure. He was working me fully out, and I had no desire to fight it. I rode his hand with like it was a dick! I was sweating, grunting, having my hair pulled and loving every second of every stroke. Each time he pushed his fingers deeper inside me, I felt myself getting closer to the feeling of cumming. I could taste, hear, and smell it; I didn't even see the room the same way. My movements were instinctual. I felt myself opening up. The sensation became almost unbearable. My anticipation increased as I felt my walls tremble. Something that felt like a lightning bolt shot up my back. But, just as soon as it came, the feeling went away. We had two good rounds of passionate body banging sex and passed out in each other's arms.

We must have been more tired than we thought. I woke up at 2:10pm and he was sound asleep snoring. I slipped out of bed and went into the bathroom to take a shower. While the water was running hot, I stepped back out to retrieve some toiletries from my suitcase. I unzipped my black luggage and immediately knew I unzipped the wrong one. My eyes were wide as I looked down at three big guns, two were black and one was silver, next to two wrapped packages of white powder. I knew exactly what it was; cocaine. I zipped his bag with my heartbeat racing and rushed back into the bathroom. My mind was going a thousand miles an hour. Were we here on drug business? Apparently so. What kind of fucking man would take a chick on a drug deal mission in another state? I was becoming more pissed instead of scared. That nigga still sleeping. I'm here in New York and he got hella drugs and three damn guns up in here with us! I was washing my body so vigorously my skin started to burn. I let the water flow over me then I stepped out. He was standing there. Right outside of the shower and startled the hell out of me.

"So did you find what you was looking for?" He asked arrogantly. I didn't know how to reply but I started talking anyway. "I wasn't looking for anything. I thought I was opening my bag. They both are black and I did see your paraphernalia but I'm not interested in it.," I managed say, knowing I was saying the wrong shit.

"Bitch I didn't ask what the fuck you were interested in, I fucking asked did you find what the fuck you was looking for?"

I was appalled at his remark. Did he think I was snooping?

"It was an honest mistake. I promise I wasn't looking in your bag!" I raised my voice a bit. The burning across my face was so intense it took me a few seconds to realize he slapped the shit out of me! I couldn't believe it. No fucking man had ever hit me before and it wasn't going to start now. I hadn't even noticed the words he was saying but the end words "Now try me if you want, bitch" felt like a sharp knife went through me. He walked out the bathroom and I stood there letting tears roll down my face. "Get it together, Tasha", I thought, "Don't let him see you cry." I looked in the mirror and I could see the handprint on my left cheek from his large right hand. He really slapped the horse shit out of me. And I let him. I wrapped myself in a oversized towel and walked out. He was in the doorway talking to someone and after the door shut, I saw that he had ordered room service. I didn't have an appetite. Nate acted as if he didn't just slap me. He was eating a burger and fries and had ordered the same for me. Once he saw that I wasn't eating he spoke. "Bitch I don't believe in wasting food so you can eat it now or eat it later, but trust me, you will eat it." He spoke sternly. I picked up the burger and obeyed. My mind was full of questions. Why was he being so evil? Did he bring me here to harm me? Did he think I was trying to steal from him? I wanted to talk but I was frightened. I finished up my burger and managed to eat a few of the fries hoping he was satisfied with my intake.

Nate came out of the bathroom fully dressed and looking clean as usual. He came over and stood in front of me. I flinched as if he was going to hit me again. He kissed my forehead gently and said, "I'll be back shortly. Be dressed. We're going shopping and I got a few ideas of what I'd like to see you in." I tried to smile, softly saying, and "Okay I'll be ready."

The weekend went by fast. After we shopped on Saturday, we had dinner at a lavish restaurant and went to the movies. We both fell asleep during the movie since we exhausted ourselves with all that shopping and Sunday afternoon we were back on the road to Baltimore. We stopped at The Home Depot and he got an extra key made for my apartment. I had no objections, he said he'll take care of the rent and he just needed to chill in the city sometimes. Maybe that passion mark I seen was from a bitch from the past, cause the whole time in New York, I did notice he wasn't talking to any bitches. Overall, Nate was a good guy. I decided I would just have to help him control his anger. I must admit, the boy knew how to spoil a girl. The overview of my trip purchases showed that. I got two pair of City boots, red and blue, a pair of black Rider boots, two jean outfits, one was ripped up and my ass cheeks hung out the bottom, a red leather coat that matched my boots to perfection, a blue leather motorcycle jacket with zippers, this bad ass body suit he picked that accentuated my breasts, waist and hips and three new bags; a Fendi purse, an MCM clutch and Louis Vuitton backpack. That slap cost him a good three grand.

FML: FUCK MY LIFE
A novel by *Mimi Ray*

Unwelcome Guest

Chink was happy to see me when I got back in town. I bought him two pair of Jordan's and two hats to match and he acted like it was Christmas. I was glad to be back home and even more glad that the slap mark had faded on my face.

I was relaxing in the bubble bath when Chink yelled for me, "big sis, come here I'm scared!" I could hear the scared tone in his voice so I hopped out the tub dripping wet and ran to his room still naked. "What's wrong?" I asked, seeing him standing there with his pants down. "Look! Help me!" He exclaimed, "It's little bugs on me!" I got closer to his private area to see what he was pointing at and I couldn't see shit. I started to think he was hallucinating then I saw it! Tiny little brown bugs crawling on his thin pubic hair.

"What the hell is that?" I asked him, knowing damn well he didn't know either. "Oh shit! These are crabs!" I answered myself. "Did you have sex? Did you fuck somebody? Are you a virgin?" I was tossing questions at Chink and he started to cry. I had no idea what to do about crabs but I didn't want them nasty little things all over the apartment. I pulled his pants up, told him to go to the car, while I threw on a sweat suit with no underclothes.

FML: FUCK MY LIFE
A novel by *Mimi Ray*

When we pulled up to Johns Hopkins Emergency Room, I could see it was live. It looked like every damn body in Baltimore had an emergency. After I parked in a decent parking spot, I told Chink to sit down while I registered him. The receptionist was pleasant but her breath smelled like shit. I felt like I was going to need a doctor too.

After three hours they finally called Chink and I to the back. The doctor was a young Asian guy, Dr. Ying, and I could barely understand his questions. He did a few tests on Chink, he confirmed that the nasty bugs was crabs and also said he had Chlamydia. My mind was racing and I was asking Chink a boat load of questions but he wouldn't give me no answers. He kept saying, "I don't know" and I was getting upset. I knew he was scared but he needed to tell us who he had sex with. The doctor left the room and I thought about taking Chink and leaving. Everything was in my head and I was sure Dr.Ying was going to call the police. Just as I told Chink to get his coat, Dr.Ying walked back in with a well dressed; big haired, older lady who looked like she meant business. She introduced herself as Mrs. Watson, a social worker for Child Protective Services. I knew we wasn't leaving just yet but I didn't know what they were planning to do.

FML: FUCK MY LIFE
A novel by *Mimi Ray*

Unexpected

"I don't even know why I came to work today," I said to Zena, my coworker as we sat in the waitress suite. Business was rather slow for a Thursday night. "What's up Tasha? talk to me," she said. "Well remember when I went to New York with Nate? While we were there, he hit me. I felt like I could forgive him since he didn't really do any harm. Then my brother was taken by Child Protective Services because he tested positive for Chlamydia and he wouldn't talk to us about it. I'm feeling fucked up for real. I just don't know what to do from here," I talked softly. "Wow Tasha, I had no idea, babes," she said with a concerned tone, "after work, Calvin and I are going for a drink, you should come, get your mind off things", she continued."You know what, I think a drink may be what I need, count me in," I told her. Nate usually didn't come over on Thursdays, so I had nothing to rush home for.

I was glad that my work uniform was all black because when we arrived at Joby's, a local lounge, I scoped some sexy eye candy. Even though that's not what I was there for, I always wanted to look my best. You never know if your next man might be there. Calvin picked a booth for us, midsection, towards the bar and with a view of the big screen.

FML: FUCK MY LIFE
A novel by *Mimi Ray*

Since I wasn't big on drinking, I ordered an Amaretto Sour, "That should keep me mellow," I thought. Zena was a drinker, she ordered a Long Island Iced Tea and Calvin had a Baltimore Zoo. That's one drink I never liked, I can't even tolerate the smell of beer let alone the taste.

We made small talk. I could tell Zena wanted me to discuss my problems more but at that point I wasn't feeling up for discussion. We talked about people at the lounge, Zena commented on a few chicks' asses and Calvin seemed to be flirting with her. That's when it dawned on me that they probably had something going on but I didn't ask. I just watched their interaction. Somehow Zena convinced me to take two shots of vodka. The first one burned like hell and I immediately wished I hadn't drank it. After I started feeling warm and cozy, I openly accepted the second shot without a second thought. I wasn't sure of the feeling that I was feeling but it was new and enlightening. It was kind of warm and tingly. The music sounded clearer and my body felt lighter.

I stood up to dance but my legs felt like rubber and I fell onto Calvin's lap almost falling on the floor. I remember him mumbling something about me not being able to drive like that, then him and Zena walking me out the lounge. My head was cloudy but I was aware. Calvin assisted me into his front seat and fastened my seatbelt. Zena was asking me was I ok and I was saying, "Yes, I'm fine," not sure as to why she was asking me that, but she took my keys and drove my car. After a quick ten or fifteen minute drive, we were parking at a two story row home on a one way street.

They both seemed to be so helpful, assisting me with my clothes and since I felt so limp, I didn't mind at all. Once again, I was pantyless, my favorite way to be, so when Zena pulled my pants down I felt bad that my pussy was so close to her face. I knew I smelled fresh, because freshness was my motto, but still, no bitch would put her pussy in my face.

I hadn't immediately noticed that Zena had already taken my shirt and bra off, but I slowly began to realize that I was naked. I just wanted to lie down and whosever bedroom we were in, I wanted to be in their bed. I felt the pillows under my head and the softness under my ass. Yes, this bed felt good and so did the nibbling on my nipples. Yea, that's exactly what it was, nibbling, and damn it felt good. I reached with my hands to feel for their head and the long flowing curls let me know it was Zena. Damn is this supposed to feel good? She's a bitch like me! It really did feel good and she could tell I liked it because while I was moaning loudly, she was nibbling harder. I felt her warm tongue on my belly, as she was kissing me lightly all over, moving between my belly and my thighs. I would never admit it, but I was so fucking aroused. It took only a second before Zena took notice. Her eyes diverted down, and back to meet mine. She had a wide toothy grin, before she leaned in to whisper to me, "I can smell your excitement, if you know what I mean." As I turned to look at her, she again licked her lips. Her finger that was tracing down my chest skipped the rest of its journey and dove into my pussy. I was soaked and her finger slide deeply into me so easily. She pulled out and her finger was dripping with my cum. Calvin was frozen in place still, not being dismissed yet. She looked at him; finger outstretched towards him and said "Do you want the first taste?" His mouth engulfed her finger and he moaned his approval as he sucked it in. Zena ran her hand over his rippled stomach and grabbed at his dick. The outline of his dick through his pants was impressive. As she stroked him her other hand returned to my pussy. I could feel my eyes half shut as she fingered me. She had other ideas though, "Keep your eyes open. Watch, see everything," she said. She teased my thighs for a few minutes and my excitement was building. As soon as her lips touched my clit, an explosion of wetness dripped out of me. This familiar feeling felt better than ever. Damn she was so gentle. It felt right. I opened my legs wider. I wanted her to keep licking my pussy. Damn she was good at it. Bitch or not she was doing it better than any man had. I felt like I was gonna piss, and I pushed her head, "Zena that's enough, I'm gonna pee!" Still slurping "Let it go baby, let it go," was her reply. She kept licking and sucking my pussy and as much as I didn't want to disrespect her and piss in her face, I was letting it go. Once it started flowing, it was magnificent. I never had a piss that felt that way. It didn't feel like it came from my bladder. It felt fucking breathtaking. It felt mind blowing. It felt exhilarating. I can't even explain how it felt but I felt like the weight of the world was lifted off my shoulders. That was the best orgasm I had experienced in my life and before I could bask in it, I felt Calvin's dick on my lips.

Calvin's dick was short and fat, like a can of soda. I managed somehow to get it into my mouth. After a few minutes of struggling, I was sucking his dick like the champ I am. And once again Zena was eating my pussy. We all had a natural connection going, all in tune with one another. Zena started fingering my pussy slowly as she continued sucking my clit and I could feel another orgasm building up. Calvin's dick was pulsating and as soon as I thought he was about to cum he pulled his dick away from me. Damn I was let down, I had a flashback of Nate shooting cum on my face and I was eagerly awaiting Calvin to do the same. Calvin had other intentions, as he was now directing us to create a new position.

FML: FUCK MY LIFE
A novel by *Mimi Ray*

My ass was high in the air as my back was arched with my stomach towards the bed. I knew he was planning to fuck me from behind and after I heard the condom wrapper being ripped I was all for it. I didn't have a view of Zena, and I started to think she left the room. I felt fingers rubbing my clit as I was bent over, doggy style. The fingers felt good and I was getting wetter and wetter. Then I felt the lips. The same soft lips as before. Damn I never imagined a woman's lips to feel so good on my pussy. I was slowly grinding Zena's face and she didn't seem to mind. In fact she wrapped her hands around my waist and was slowly face fucking me. Damn she was experienced! I was sure she would drown from all my wetness but she was swallowing it up without hesitation. I felt the pressure of Calvin's body on my ass and Zena continued doing her thing. I prepared for mounting and held my breath. I felt the thickness of Calvin's dick stretching my pussy, but as long as Zena's mouth was on my clit, I was sure I could handle this extreme satisfaction. Calvin fucked my pussy as if it belonged to him. He was panting and breathing hard and with each pant his dick went deeper. Damn it was feeling so good. Lips on my clit and a dick in my pussy. I didn't want the feeling to stop but my legs started shaking, my body started trembling, my teeth started chattering and I felt my eyes bulging! Whatever the hell was happening, my goodness, it

FML: FUCK MY LIFE
A novel by *Mimi Ray*

felt like I was on a rocket taking off into outer space. Every square foot of my body was experiencing pleasure together and all I could do was cry. Tears from pleasure filled the pillow beneath my face and my whole body fell limp. Holy fucking shit! I could get so used to this!

Whatever they were doing to each other after I climaxed, didn't include me. I was out for the count and although I could hear Zena moaning, it sounded like a musical lullaby sending me off to dreamland. I pulled up to my apartment building and to my surprise Nate's car was parked directly out front. That wasn't like him to come over on Thursday nights, and he hadn't even paged me to let me know he was there. I walked up the stairs leading to my apartment feeling sluggish from the aftermath of great sex. My legs felt like jello and I felt my knees threaten to give way with each step. It was 5:30 in the morning and I knew Nate was going to be heated. I mentally prepared myself for another slap that I was sure to receive from not being there. To be honest the night I had was worth the agony I was sure to endure. I kept replaying the scenes over and over. And I was fully satisfied, even if that meant I was bisexual now. As I approached the door what I knew was waiting on the other side became a reality and I felt instantly drained. I put my key in the lock and turned it as quietly as I could; hoping and praying Nate would be asleep. As I quietly pushed the door open an inch, it was yanked open from the other side and my prayers of Nate being asleep was wishful thinking. Before I could open my mouth to utter a convincing lie that I hadn't yet thought of, I felt the powerful blow of his fist connect with the side of my face. The force of the blow sent me flying backwards into the wall. My head hit the wall with such force, my teeth rattled and I bit my tongue so hard my mouth was instantly filled with the hot sticky metallic taste of my own blood. Something in me snapped and in that moment I vowed on my life that this nigga would pay with his fucking life!

FML: FUCK MY LIFE
A novel by *Mimi Ray*

Family Affair

Kashay was turning one and everyone was invited to come to her 1st birthday party. Worm and Tammy rented a community hall and was going above and beyond to make sure their princess had an outstanding time. They rented a moon bounce, hired a clown and Barney the Dinosaur was there. I was impressed. Tammy didn't have a job so I knew Worm was selling drugs for sure now. I couldn't be upset. He didn't finish school. He really didn't have any role models besides me. And who was I? A "drop-out" too. Yea I got my GED but my highest level of education was two months of ninth grade plus I had skipped the third grade and I was naturally smart. He didn't have any skills and no one really taught him better. I guess he was doing what he had to do to take care of his family and from the protrusion in Tammy's' stomach, I already made up my mind that she must be pregnant again. I'll ask her later, at the party, wasn't a good time. Besides it's all about Kashay today. I was having such a good time playing with the kids that I even allowed the clown to paint my face.

As I was walking towards the bathroom to look in the mirror, I saw Chink coming in the door, with Mrs. Watson beside him. I was so damn happy! I ran over and hugged Chink and he hugged me back

with the same enthusiasm. Mrs. Watson said that
Chink was granted two hours to be with the family
and she would pick him up at 5pm. I thanked her
and turned to talk to Chink, but he had already been
taken by everyone to talk, laugh and catch up. I
proceeded to the bathroom to look at my face paint
and down the corridor I could see Worm talking
with two people. "Come here Tasha," Worm yelled
and motioned for me to come. I walked towards the
three of them but by the time I reached them, the
taller one had walked away. I looked at the other
person, and was surprised to see our mother, Pam.
She looked the same; frail and sickly and her skin
had gotten darker. Before I even got a chance to
speak, Worm started talking. "Listen y'all, it's my
daughters' birthday. I want everyone to get along.
Tasha I know you don't like being around mommy
but she's still our mother. I've been helping her out
and she's going to rehab soon. I've been keeping my
eye on her and she's not as bad as she was." He
talked without stopping, "if mommy is gonna get
high, she's gonna get high. We can't stop her and
excluding her from the family doesn't make It no
better. Whenever she feels she needs a hit, she gets
it from me and it's usually enough to keep her on
the right track," he continued and I was finally
understanding what was happening. "So Tasha, get
used to seeing her around, because I've forgiven her
and I'm going to help her get clean." I was taken

aback, allowing my mind to process what I heard and just to be sure I was hearing it right I said, "So Pam wants to get clean, and you're going to help her by giving her drugs?" I didn't wait for an answer, I said, "Good luck with that," then I turned and walked away. As I was walking back towards the party, I heard Pam say, "Thanks Worm, I won't let you down."

I wanted to believe in Pam, but past experiences wouldn't allow me to. I guess Worm will see the hard way. I wished Booker was there. He hadn't replied to my last letter, and I mailed it three weeks ago.

Kashay had loads of fun at her party. After they opened the gifts, I started giving hugs and saying goodbyes and took note that it was time for Chink to leave with Ms. Watson. I had hoped to question him some more but I looked to be out of time.

FML: FUCK MY LIFE
A novel by *Mimi Ray*

Nate's Gift

We were coming up on our two year anniversary and I really couldn't complain about a thing. Nate practically moved in and I was an assistant manager at Bob Big Boys. Every chance I got I was enjoying Zena eating my pussy and I never considered it cheating because she was a chick like me. Being with Zena was an escape from reality. Although Nate had slacked up on whooping my ass, I still caught the rapture whenever he was stressed. Calvin still flirted but he once remarked that he was staying away from me since I continued to stay with my "crazy" boyfriend. Zena was really the only home girl I had and Nate approved of her because all she did was work and I lied and told him that she went to church twice a week. Little white lies didn't hurt anyone. Besides, I knew Nate wasn't a saint but he kept the rent paid, food in the house and he still provided me with the best dick of my life. If only I could have a session with Zena and Nate, I would consider life close to perfect. However I knew that would never happen. Nate was possessive over me and he once told me that he never wanted another man's hands on my body and for my health I better not want another man's hands on me. I didn't even have enough courage in me to ask him if that was the same thoughts he had about a females hands.

I was vacuuming the living room carpet with the music blasting and just a pair of yellow thongs on when Nate came home with four Mexican guys. I couldn't even ask a question because I ran so fast to get some clothes on before that earned me an ass whooping. While getting dressed, I could hear Nate telling them, "only the TV's and dining room furniture, leave everything else." I managed to slip on leggings and a tank top and hauled ass back in the living room. "Nate what is going on?" I asked, being sure not to raise my voice past his approval level. "We are moving to the county baby, and I suggest you to pack your own jewelry and China," he smiled. He had one hell of a way of surprising me. I didn't think of another question, I went and did as he suggested, being sure to wrap my delicate things in blankets before placing them in bags.

The Mexican guys did as they were told under direction of Nate. They arranged everything the way he wanted and he kissed me and left with them. "I'll be back with dinner," was all he said right before he shut the door. The new place was a two bedroom, two bathroom condominium in White Marsh, a county outside of east Baltimore. He had already purchased new furniture and a new bedroom set. I knew he wouldn't take the bed that Scooter and I used to sleep on. Even though he stopped making comments a long time ago, I remember him asking me "If he was to die would I fuck a man in his bed?" I chuckled thinking of how slick-mouthed Nate could be at times.

I started putting some of my clothes away in the closet closest to the window since I saw that Nate had already chosen his closet by the thirty or so shoe boxes lined across the wall. I took note of how quiet it was, even with the bedroom window opened, I didn't hear a fire truck, police car or kids playing in the street. "I could get used to this," I thought as I made my way around our new condo.

During my tour of the new place, I was opening all the doors, which revealed closets of all sizes. It was another door which sat off the living room that I thought could be a boiler room so I saved that for last. I opened the door and to my astonishment, it was decorated for a baby. Pink and yellow decorations hung and a big pretty crib with the inscription "Natalia" printed in gold letters across it. My first thought was, "Did Nate think I was pregnant?" My second thought was, "Natalia?" My mind was racing. And before I could even think of my next thought, Nate walked in with a baby girl about nine months old in his arms and said, "Tasha, come here, my daughter is going to live with us."

FML: FUCK MY LIFE
A novel by *Mimi Ray*

It's Over

I felt like I was living a dream, a cruel nightmare to be exact. "The audacity of Nate to move me to a nice new condo and expect me to accept a baby I never knew he had. If my calculations were correct, he must have been fucking some bitch six months into our relationship and she birthed this bastard child. She was named after him. She looked like him. He was connected to that baby. He probably was with the mother throughout the pregnancy. Who the hell is the mother? Why the fuck do she got to live here?" I knew Nate did his dirt in the streets. A few times I suspected he was cheating but I never had any concrete evidence. And even if I did have evidence, I probably wouldn't have approached him with it. As long as it wasn't in my face, I pretended it never happened. Besides, I got a good deal from the relationship. I was pissed to the highest level of pisstivity. I felt no connection to that child. "How dare him, nonchalantly introducing me to a got damn fucking baby that he shouldn't even have! Did he really think I would go for this shit? I fucking hate him and I'm getting the fuck away from him as soon as he closes his eyes. Him and that baby can have this whole damn place to themselves. He likes to flash money. He likes to play rich. He can hire a damn nanny for it." All these thoughts were in my head but not a word was coming out of my mouth. I was stunned. I was heartbroken. And I was torn. I kept thinking where did things go wrong and all I could come up with was New York City a couple years ago. I should have left Nate then and never looked back. He's never going to change. A damn woman beating, cheating, manipulating coward ass bitch. He must have put a damn spell on me cause I never been a sucker like this before. I haven't been to see Booker. I missed Chinks weekly calls for the last two months. I hadn't seen Kashay or Worm in about four months. All for some dick. I really need to get my life together. And I will. Cause I'm leaving this bastard ASAP. No turning back!!

FML: FUCK MY LIFE
A novel by *Mimi Ray*

Emotions

It had been three days since I packed up my stuff that was barely unpacked and returned to my old apartment while Nate and Natalia were asleep. I had my locks changed and I purchased a .22 revolver from off the block. It wasn't any trouble at all getting the gun. All I did was flash the money and the young corner hustler returned with the piece. I was serious about keeping Nate away from me. It was all good just a week ago but was it really? I was tired of tip toeing around my own place; watching what I say, jumping when he came too close, and pretending! Hell no it wasn't all good. Fuck Nate! I swear I will shoot his ass. But from the looks of things, he didn't seem to care that I was gone. It's been three days. No paging me. No calling me. No knock at the door. Maybe everything was a fake ass lie for the last two years. Apparently so; he must have had two lives. Am I the other woman? My mind was all over the place like a bipolar maniac. Shit, fuck him! I'm not his woman. I'm going to get me some dick! This is my pussy and someone will appreciate what that deadbeat bastard didn't.

I found myself walking into Joby's lounge after driving for an hour with no definite destination in mind. I hadn't been there in so long, but the decor was the same. I ordered a drink, a Motherfucker, and sat at the bar alone. It burned as it touched my parched throat. And as soon as it was gone I ordered another one. This time I sipped slowly. I was replaying everything that happened over the last week, and I didn't know if I was happy or sad, mad or glad. I was fucked up. I felt tears on my cheeks and I hadn't realized I was crying.

"Tasha, I hadn't expected to see you here," a familiar voice said. I looked up and it was Calvin. I tried to hide my tears and smile but he had already started wiping my face with a napkin. "Don't cry baby, it will be ok," he whispered; that just made me cry harder. I fell into his arms and I felt so safe. He allowed me to cry on his chest for a few minutes; then I controlled myself and sat up. "Thanks," I said. He smiled."Come on, I'll take you home," he offered. "I need to be held, take me with you," I practically begged. "That's fine, I'll drive your car, you're in no shape to drive." I nodded my head, agreeing, and handed him my keys.

Calvin and I wasted no time attacking each other. It was like we were two teens finally getting what they had been forbidden to do. We kissed and caressed each other and was sucking and fucking all over the place like a roller coaster ride. Up, down, flips, flops, on the bed, on the dresser, on the floor, in every position manageable. I sucked his dick like it was the last dick on earth and he made love to me like I was his wedded wife. It was passionate, rough, gentle, then hard and all mixed with emotions. Maybe he was going through something too, because we barely talked, but we understood everything the other one said.

FML: FUCK MY LIFE
A novel by *Mimi Ray*

Plotting

I still felt tipsy after leaving Calvin's house but I wanted to go home and be alone with my thoughts. I couldn't take my mind off the night's events all I could think of was when we could get together and do it again. As I stuck my key in the lock I realized the door was already unlocked. I instantly sobered up thinking who the fuck could be in my apartment! As I slowly entered I saw Nate pacing back and forth rubbing his hands over his head frantically. He looked like a crazed man and hadn't even realized I was present. As he turned to pace in the opposite direction the light hit his face in such a way that I noticed what appeared to be dry caked up blood on the side of his head with traces down his neck and on his diamond encrusted chain. I rushed toward him full of concern. I had to grab him to get his attention, "Baby!" I exclaimed, "What the hell happened? Are you alright? What the fuck!" My words were coming out at lightning speed. Before he could answer one question, I was firing another. I instantly felt guilty. While I was out getting my back blown out the man I loved was hurting. Nothing else mattered at that moment. Not even the baby. I felt so bad. He turned to me and hugged me so tight I could barely breathe "Tasha," He said, his voice laced with desperation "I need you baby, I need your help." At that moment I would have done anything to help him. He began to tell me how the transaction between him and a dude he was used to dealing with went way wrong. I didn't know much of his business or who he associated with in the streets and he didn't go into detail not even then. He just kept repeating. "I can't believe Rich, not my boy! Rich was suppose to be my man," as he was rambling I just held his head to my breast and rocked him back and forth, cooing "shh shh," trying to comfort him in the only way I knew how besides sucking his dick and that just didn't seem like the answer at this time. Thoughts of me sucking Calvin's dick flooded my mind and in that instant, I felt like shit. I felt like a whore, like trash, as worthless as my mother. While she was a whore for drugs I was a whore for money and with all the ass I've sold I still couldn't save my brothers. One by one they fell and silent tears ran continuously down my face.

Nate looked up with a look on his face like whatever demons he was fighting, he saw a way out. He began talking so fast. I just stood nodding my head like an idiot agreeing to whatever he was saying. He told me his homeboy Rich, who I'd only met once, but remembered because he was hella fine. I remembered thinking I'd ride his sexy ass three ways til Tuesday and twice on Sundays. I had to force myself to focus on what Nate was saying as he explained Rich had apparently set him up and he and the dude they were doing business with robbed him. He started to formulate a plan and ask if I would be down with him. He said that he loved me and what he needed me to do would save his life or keep him out of prison. I was raised by the motto ride or die, so of course I was with it. Plus the guilt I felt just wouldn't let up. After I felt things would be ok with Nate's plan, immediately my thoughts returned to Calvin and a slight smirk begin to play at the corners of my mouth.

FML: FUCK MY LIFE
A novel by *Mimi Ray*

The Set Up

The following Friday my nerves was at an all-time high. The day had come when I was supposed to meet Rich, get him to the hotel and assist in him being robbed. Nate had mapped everything out. He knew Rich's schedule very well, from his barbershop appointment that morning, to him dropping off his son at his moms at 4pm, to his large money pick up at 8pm, before he headed to his weekly escapade at Norma Jeans Strip Club, which was where I was supposed to meet him. Nate explained how faithfully every Friday, Rich picked up a different chick from the club and took her to Quality Estates Hotel on South Broadway. Tonight, I was to be sure to be that girl. He went on to say Rich would be intrigued with me since I fit the description of his usual choice of chicks, 5'5", brown skin, pretty teeth with a nice body, flat stomach and phat ass but most importantly unfamiliar. He didn't think Rich would recall that he had seen me once, since he smoked weed regularly and since then I had dyed my hair with burgundy streaks. I prayed Nate was right, so Rich would take me as the bait. And although I was nervous and needed a shot of Vodka, I also needed to keep a clear head to get through this.

FML: FUCK MY LIFE
A novel by *Mimi Ray*

I was dressed in a short cream leather dress with chocolate thigh high boots with studs on the heels. My breasts were sitting high and my ass was perfectly rounded as the leather grabbed it tightly. My skin and hair was flawless but that was the usual. I added an extra touch of makeup and sprayed my "Cum Fuck Me" perfume and out the door I went. I had to admit if I was Rich, I would want to fuck me too. Everything was well organized, down to the cab waiting out front. Nate didn't want me to drive. He wanted me to "need" Rich. He had given me a prepaid cell and I was to send the room number to his pager and do whatever it took to keep Rich occupied until he get there. The plan was that Nate would come in masked, get Rich's keys and get to his trunk where everything would be waiting to be taken. Nate mapped it out so well, I knew it had to go smoothly.

It was 1:00 am and I was doing perfect. I caught Rich's attention from the moment he came in by tossing my ass around and dancing flirtatiously. He hadn't left my side since introducing himself, so I knew I was his choice of the night. We made small talk; I told him my name was Star and he had said it over twenty times so far. "Star baby, you're so fine, what can I get you, are you here alone, Sexy Star you're like a dream come true." He was throwing it on heavy and maybe an ordinary bitch would have been wetting her panties, but I was here on business and those compliments meant diddly. I could tell he was ready to go, once he whispered in my ear, "Let's finish this elsewhere, I'll pay for your time," I smiled as if he was on the right track and followed his lead.

Just as Nate had presumed, we were parking at Quality Estates Hotel and once Rich came back to the car to get me, I followed him to the room; Room 235. Rich was definitely fine as fuck and if things had been different I would have fucked him willingly, free of charge. As soon as he went into the bathroom, I unlocked the door, and paged Nate, with the room 235. Then put the cell in my purse and my purse under my jacket.

I was hoping Nate arrived quickly so I didn't have to get far, like getting naked, but already an hour had passed since I paged him and Rich was getting more and more touchy. I was playing the shy girl role but I could see his patience was wearing thin. He said, "Lay back let me undress you." I started to panic; my eyes shifted side to side, my heart started to pound in my throat. I was thinking where the hell was Nate? I kept saying over and over to myself "stay calm, stay cool, bitch, play your position!" But inside I was anything but calm. I stalled long enough trying to distract Rich licking my lips, moving really slow, pretending to be seductive when I was actually trying to buy by some fucking time. I felt like Nate's ass left me to fend for myself while I was trying to do his ass a fucking favor. At this point I had to save my own ass. I couldn't blow my cover; I couldn't do anything but go with the flow. I slowly lifted my hips as Rich slid my chocolate see-through Victoria Secret thong over my hips. Looking down at his pretty ass looking up at me I instantly started to get moist and thought to myself playing my position didn't seem so bad after all. I began to relax and really get into seducing dude... no acting necessary. Nigga was straight fine! Rich wasted no time burying his face between my legs and I must say he knew how to eat pussy that's for sure. In no time my toes were curling inside my thigh high boots that I'd left on since I'd always wanted to get fucked in some sexy ass boots. This seemed the night I would get to do a few things I always wanted to do. Before I knew it my legs were shaking so hard I began to wrap my legs tighter around Rich's neck as my orgasm intensified my thighs had him in a vice grip. I was lost in a world of complete ecstasy as wave after wave of intense pleasure took over me. Finally I was spent. Rich was lying still, head still buried in my thick thighs. Panting, I asked, "was it as good for you as it was for me?" when he didn't answer I gently nudge him. When he didn't budge I jumped up as I pushed him off of me. His eyes were wide open but he didn't appear to be seeing and didn't look like he was breathing. I began calling his name and shaking him vigorously, "Rich! Rich!" when he didn't respond I felt his neck for a pulse like they always do on TV. I didn't feel shit that's when I knew that nigga was dead. I grabbed my shit, and hauled ass. Just as I had my hand on the hotel door I remembered you're suppose to wipe shit down, leave no trace. Those hours of watching TV was good for something. I took a towel from the hotel bathroom and wiped off everything I touched even Rich's mouth! No DNA was gonna be left to lead the police back to me. I may be young but I damn sure ain't stupid! I stuffed my thong in my boots and grabbed his keys, turned the door knob, this time with the towel and stuffed the towel in my purse. I rushed to Rich's car and as I tried to unlock the door I dropped the keys my hands were shaking so bad, I finally was able to get in the car and began to drive away. I was driving for about twenty minutes when I pulled into an abandoned alley. I had no idea where I was but I saw traffic lights and what looked like a gas station not too far away, maybe about a block and a half up the road. I took the towel and repeated the wipe down ritual I perfected in the hotel before I popped the trunk, just to make sure that I wasn't leaving anything of value in the car. The trunk was empty except for a black duffle bag nestled in the corner. I grabbed the bag and unzipped it. My mouth fell wide open and for a second I forgot where I was and all the events that transpired. Inside the bag was more money than I had ever seen in my entire life plus two guns. The sight of the guns quickly snapped me out of my trances. I hurriedly zipped the bag threw it over my shoulder and walked away as calm as I could. I kept looking over my shoulder to make sure that I wasn't being followed and no one saw me. I was straight paranoid! As I passed a dumpster I threw the keys inside and continued to walk toward the gas station. Once I made it to the gas station I calmed a little. No one was paying me any attention and I had to remind myself that only I knew what had just happened. People were pumping gas, buying cigarettes and in general, going about their business. I flagged a taxi and took my paranoid ass home.

Things Change

It was 6pm the following evening, I had no intent on going to work and I had yet to hear from Nate. The sensitive part of me was worried and scared wondering if something had happened to him and the cold-hearted part of me was frustrated and angry, thinking that if he was okay, I was going to hold him at gun point and demand answers. I was beginning to trust no one. Maybe he had set me up and planned to destroy me along with Rich. The devil was whispering in my ear and my mind was playing tricks on me. Not knowing where Nate was at or what he was up to kept me on edge. I had counted the money three times and it was close to $20, 000. I had replayed what happened over and over and had decided that I would tell Nate that Rich had fallen asleep once we got to the hotel and I escaped unharmed. I wouldn't tell him I fucked Rich or that he wasn't breathing when I left. Right now, Nate was the missing piece of the puzzle that I was creating in my brain, and until I had answers to my questions, not even Nate was safe from my premeditated thoughts. I was still hurting over the fact that Nate had a baby and it's been two weeks and he hadn't addressed that situation at all. "I did all the work, so I should keep all the damn money. What Nate won't know won't hurt him," I was selfishly thinking. "Maybe Nate decided to be with his daughter's mother," my mind began to wander and before the next thought entered my mind, the phone rang, distracting me from my thoughts.

I jumped off the sofa fast, thinking it could be Nate. "Hello?" I said into the telephone receiver, anxiously listening for the callers' voice. "Tasha, its Worm, meet me at Johns Hopkins Hospital, mommy just got rushed by ambulance!" Without hesitation, I dropped the phone and ran to my room to get dressed. Every horrible thought imaginable was flashing across my brain. I wished that I had asked Worm more questions so I could have better prepared for whatever was happening. Was it an accident? Did she have a heart attack? Did she overdose? I ran back to the phone and called Worm back, but got no answer. I grabbed my purse, the prepaid cell and my keys and ran out to my car with quickness.

Worm must had called the whole family. When I got off the elevator on the fourth floor, as the receptionist had directed me to, I saw family members that I hadn't seen in months. The only time that many people came to the hospital is when someone is dead or near death. I began to think the worst and I felt nauseated. Although she wasn't the best mother, or even a good mother, to lose your mother is devastating, I imagined it would be anyway. Tammy, noticeably pregnant and looking like she was ready to deliver, was rushing towards me talking but I could barely understand her rambling. But when she said, "Even Booker and Chink are on their way." I asked Tammy to slow down and tell me what had happened. She went on explaining that my mother was in a coma, side effects from taking a lethal drug overdose and the doctors was not sure if she was strong enough to pull through. She continued, saying Kashay had found her in their bathroom, foaming at the mouth, convulsing and bleeding with a needle sticking out of her arm and that she was pretty shaken up from that sight. I gathered my strength and walked towards the room my mother was admitted to. Scattered around looking helpless was her estranged older brother, I hadn't seen in years, as well as a tall thin man that I didn't recognize, my grandparents looking drunk and careless and Worm with dark bags under his eyes. I walked over to her bedside and she looked pitiful. Several dark spots covered her face, neck and ears, her eyes were sunken and she even shaved her hair off wearing a short afro. Worm stood beside me and as he put his heavy muscular arm around my shoulders, he whispered, "I tried big sis, I really tried," I could see the pain in his eyes.

There was a knock on the door and we both turned simultaneously to see who was walking in; it was Booker. He was escorted by an officer but he wasn't handcuffed. He had gotten taller, at least 5'8" now and you could see muscle prints under his plain yellow jumpsuit. He walked over to us and we hugged in a three-way hug. I felt so emotional; the tears were building up but I didn't let them fall. I wanted to help my mother but she was a failure to me. And even seeing her lying there comatose, I only felt remorse for my brothers.

I excused myself to go sit in the waiting area. I planned to leave once I saw Chink, and 15 minutes later Chink arrived with a face full of tears. I expected that though. He was the youngest and he barely understood what was going on. I grabbed him tightly and he pushed me away. I didn't expect that. He looked at me angrily then spoke in a high tone, "Don't touch me! Don't touch me! You told me you would come for me and I'm still in that foster home! You don't care about me! You only care about yourself! Even when you made me stay with Nate's sister and she made me be nasty with her daughter, you didn't care!" he screamed, "I hate you Tasha, I hate you!" My heart shattered. I couldn't believe what I was hearing. My brother was forced to sleep with Nate's niece? He blamed me for everything? Maybe it was my fault. I didn't really know Noel at the time but Chink held this secret for so long. My life seemed to be getting crazier and the words Chink said, "You only care about yourself," replayed repeatedly in my head. I grabbed my purse off the waiting room chair and aimlessly walked toward the elevator. I drove straight to Noel's house with rage boiling in my blood.

FML: FUCK MY LIFE
A novel by *Mimi Ray*

Shocked

I sped on 83 North from Johns Hopkins Hospital, racing to 695 West to 795 North, driving like a maniac. I had every intent to beat the living shit out of Noel and I contemplated going to Central Booking Holding Center that night. In my mind I had already killed her with my bare hands and left her children motherless.

I banged on Noel's door aggressively, not caring if I had disturbed her neighbors or awakened her kids. I was prepared to viciously attack her as soon as she opened the door, but when she opened it, I hadn't expected she would be holding Natalia in her arms. She looked at me as if I was the person she was expecting and said "Tasha's here now," to whomever she was talking to on the phone. I reluctantly walked in after she gestured for me to enter. "Uh huh... yea.... wow..... ok, I'll try.... yes, thanks," she said as she ended her call. She looked at me and said, rather flatly, "I was just about to call you, Nate's locked up."

"Locked up?" I asked, feeling like my lungs was caving in. "When the fuck did this happen? how?" I asked totally forgetting why I had come there. Every negative, evil and violent thought that I carried for Nate and Noel vanished. All I wanted was him to walk through the door and say "April

Fools!" But listening to Noel recount what she knew, I slowly sat down at her kitchen table and listened to her attentively as she gave the baby a bottle. Noel explained that "A friend" had called her Saturday morning saying Nate was arrested Friday night. He was found with a mask, a gun, drugs and money in his car and he was being held with no bond. She said to make matters worse; he had struck an fucking officer with his car after attempting to escape, and led the cops on a damn high speed chase. After he was apprehended, his dumb ass resisted arrest and was tackled by several officers and sustained a broken jaw and four fractured ribs.

After hearing the love of my life had been beaten by officers, I once again felt terrible for thinking he had abandoned me and even worst for not trusting him. I asked her who was "The friend" who called her, not because I was being nosey but I recalled Nate saying that Rich and another dude had set him up. He never went into any details about that other dude, but Noel's answer was definitely not related to Rich, when she simply said, "Natalia's mom, that's who I was talking to when you knocked."

I didn't want Noel to know that Nate hadn't told me about Natalia until recently. Her behaviors showed me that she obviously thought that I been knew about the baby. Casually, I prodded with my questions until I had majority of my questions answered. Natalia's mom was a friend of Noel's that Nate once dated. She had four other kids and custody of none. She got caught up with the wrong guy and became addicted to drugs and she was currently in a drug treatment center attempting to kick her habit. She agreed for Noel to keep Natalia since Nate was now locked up but never once did she say her name.

I instantaneously felt sympathy for Natalia; she was just a baby and I flash backed on my life, and thought about my mother and her ongoing drug problems. No one deserved to be born into these circumstances, I thought. I wished her well, asked her to call me with any news and quietly left her apartment much calmer than when I had arrived.

FML: FUCK MY LIFE
A novel by *Mimi Ray*

Numb

I hadn't left my apartment for over a week and I really didn't have any desire to do so. Although the phone was continuously ringing, I hadn't answered one time. I didn't know if Nate had called, or Noel or even if my mom was still in a coma. I couldn't even remember the last time I showered and although I was beginning to smell like onions and sourdough, I couldn't find the strength to groom myself. I only ate when I was extremely hungry, like every other day, and even when I ate, it was very small portions of bread, crackers and dry cereal. I felt nauseated intermittently and I went through a few two-liters of Ginger Ale, determined to nurse whatever illness had set into me.

First I thought I was heartbroken. I missed Nate intensely. I day dreamed of him walking into my bedroom, scooping me up and spinning me around after surprising me with a bouquet of roses and perfume as he had in the past. I day dreamed that he asked me to run far away with him and we lived happily ever after. The emptiness I felt in my heart was unbearable. I felt lonely and depressed and even knowing that I had almost $20,000 hidden in my closet, I still couldn't form a smile on my face. I would have gladly given up the money in exchange for Nate to be home in my arms, embracing my love, keeping me happy.

"Tasha, hello? Tasha?" I heard a voice outside my window. I knew it was Zena but before I could look out the window to tell her to go away, she was knocking at the door. "I know you're home, open up, I see your car, I've been calling you," she continued to talk into my door. She was bent on getting in so to avoid embarrassment from my neighbors, I opened the door and let her in. "Damn girl! What the hell died in here," she said, while rushing to open a window. "What the hell is going on with you? You know your ass is fired right?" I didn't answer. "Tasha have you been taking drugs?" I snapped! "Bitch don't you remember I have a crack head mother who may even be dead by now. Every got damn person in my family is a damn crack head. I don't and I won't ever in my life take drugs and if you ever ask me some shit like that again I'll show you just how much drugs I'm using when I kick your fucking ass!!" She laughed hysterically and said, "Well at least I know you're not deaf." I laid on the couch, feeling lightheaded and she rushed to my side. "Tasha seriously girl what's going on with you? Everyone is worried and now that I see you face to face, I'm worried too," Zena whispered as if someone else was in the room. "Why are you whispering? And I don't know what's wrong with me, besides my man is gone, my family

is fucked up, you just said I'm fired and ----
ouchhhh!" I screamed as a sharp pain ripped
through my side. I curled up in fetal position,
rocking myself wishing the pain would stop but it
didn't let up, it got stronger. "Zena, I think I'm
pregnant. I know I'm pregnant. Take me to the
hospital. I can't take this no more", I said between
breaths. Zena didn't ask any questions. She wrapped
a blanket around me, put my slippers on my feet,
grabbed my purse and helped me down the stairs.
By the time I made it to her car, the pain was so
excruciating that I just stopped and laid on the
ground. She helped me into the backseat and I laid
across the cold leather upholstery wishing it was all
a dream.

I woke up and adjusted my eyes. It was so
bright in the room, I'm surprised I had even fallen
asleep. I looked down at my right hand to identity
the contraption that was causing the burning
sensation I was enduring. It was an IV, and as my
eyes followed the tubing, I took note of two big
bags of fluids but only one was connected to the
tubing. Zena was watching TV, sitting next to my
bedside table and she smiled as she noticed I had
awakened. "How are you feeling?" she asked softly.
I really was unsure of how I was feeling, but I still
replied with, "I'm ok."

An older white lady, with a nurse's uniform
walked in with a small bag of fluids in her hand. I

could see her name tag, "Janet," but she didn't introduce herself. "Good to see you've awaken, I'm going to hang this antibiotic and it will run for 20 minutes," she said flatly. "Ok, that's fine; can I see the doctor please?" I asked dryly. "He's on his way," she stated as she quickly walked away. "Damn," I said to Zena, "that bitch acted like I was contagious," feeling myself catching an attitude. I felt like I had to use the bathroom so I asked Zena to spot me while I walked, just in case I felt lightheaded like I had before. As I was walking, I realized the pain that had ripped through my side was now nonexistent. A new feeling had emerged, sticky wetness between my legs. Once I reached the toilet, I looked down and just as I had suspected, my thighs were covered with a dark burgundy and bright red mixture of blood with clots as large as quarters. I started to cry, not because of the bleeding, but I presumed that I lost the fetus I was carrying. I cried because I was a mess. I just sat there on the toilet crying. And Zena did not disturb me.

FML: FUCK MY LIFE
A novel by *Mimi Ray*

Missing Person

After being discharged from Mercy Medical Center three days ago, I was beginning to feel like myself again. Besides the occasional cramps in my lower abdomen, I didn't feel like I had just went through a four day hospital stay. I thought about the miscarriage, and although I didn't really feel sad, I didn't know what I felt. I blamed myself, for ignoring another pregnancy but I was young and although my body was developed on the outside, it obviously wasn't developed on the inside. This was a silent reminder that I wasn't as grown as I thought I was.

While in the hospital I received a visit from a young social worker, Kenya Drew, and the conversation we held had me thinking intensely about my life. She had given me her business card, and I placed it in my nightstand for safekeeping once I got home. She was warmly polite and easy to talk to and she encouraged me to call her if I needed her services in the future. Kenya didn't really ask questions, she let me talk. I told her how I was feeling heartbroken and lost and how I had let Chink down without realizing it. I told her how no matter how fucking hard I tried it just seemed that I couldn't please people. She told me to face each problem and solve them, one by one, and I intended to do so.

After opening my blinds, allowing some much needed sunshine into my apartment, I decided to go to the mall. Nothing like some retail therapy to make a girls' day brighter. I went to my secret stash, counted out $5000 and thoughts of Nate and Rich entered my mind. I hadn't heard any word on Nate and surprisingly hadn't heard of any funeral talk floating around.

I sat at my folding chair, and made a mental note to purchase a high-back chair and new computer desk, as I logged onto the Internet and began to search "body found" "hotel" "Rich" "South Broadway" to see if I could gather any information. Nothing came up. I searched The Baltimore Sun Paper, the obituary section, Police Blotter and The City Paper, still, nothing came up. A worrisome feeling came over me as I began to replay the events at the hotel. I needed to find some answers and I thought of a plan. Before heading to the mall, I would go past the Police Station, and turn in a gun. There was a gun program, "No Questions Asked," where you could drop off guns without being questioned.

After cleaning off the .22 I had bought off the block, I carefully wrapped it in a small green towel and placed it in my purse. With many thoughts racing through my head, I headed out the door, in search for some answers. Shortly I arrived at the same police station I visited before for Booker. I thought about how much I missed him and decided that he would be the next person I needed to visit.

I hadn't realized that I was staring into space until an older gentleman tapped me on my shoulder snapping me out of my daze. "Hello miss, are you being helped?" he asked. "Thank you, I was looking for the Missing Person board I saw when I visited here before," I answered flatly. "Sure it's right this way, follow me." I obeyed his command and followed "Is there anyone you're looking for in particular?" he asked without turning to face me. I thought quickly and stated, "No I just thought I recognized a face and I wanted to take a closer look." "Well here you go," he said, as we stopped in front of the large bulletin board. He walked away without waiting for a "thank you."

My eyes carefully searched over each picture hoping to see Rich's face. There were people of all races and ages and some of them, I wondered, how they were connected to Baltimore. Each picture had a small snippet about each person and after thirty minutes of examining the bulletin board, I walked away empty handed. As I walked past the desk, with a large, "No Questions Asked" sign, I reached in my purse and placed the towel wrapped gun in front of the middle aged attendant and left the station.

FML: FUCK MY LIFE
A novel by *Mimi Ray*

I felt puzzled that there was no trace of Rich's death but I still had hope to find out for sure and instead of heading to the mall, I headed to Quality Estates Hotel. I played out a conversation in my head that I would attempt with the hotel attendant. Once I arrived, I went straight into acting mode. "Good," I thought, happy to see that it was a young man at the hotels' desk, "flirting shall get me some answers." As I walked towards the check-in line, I saw that I was next in line. I ran my fingers through my long wrapped hair and re-applied some lip-gloss. I noticed the desk clerk checking me out so I adjusted my shirt, revealing a nice amount of cleavage. After the older couple who was standing in front of me walked away, I flirtatiously approached the desk and said, "Room for one please."

"Sure, would you need smoking or non-smoking?" He asked while his eyes leered toward my breasts.

"It doesn't matter if it's smoking or not, as long as it's not the room that the dead man was found in!" I giggled hoping he would fall into conversation.

"Dead man?" He questioned with a puzzled look on his face.

"Yea, I heard it was a dead man found in room 235 or something, a few weeks ago, I would not want to be in that room", I said, acting as if I would be scared.

"Well I've been working here two months now and I haven't heard anything about that but I can give you a room on the fourth floor just to be sure no ghosts will get you", he laughed but I no longer needed to play along. I heard exactly what I needed to hear. "You know what, I left my ID in the car", I quickly uttered as I turned and exited the hotel.

Now my mind was really racing with outlandish thoughts. I was damn sure Rich was dead when I didn't feel a pulse. He wasn't breathing and he didn't budge when I moved him. "Could Rich be alive?" panic soared through me, "There's only one way to be sure," I thought and first thing tomorrow morning I'm going to find out.

FML: FUCK MY LIFE
A novel by *Mimi Ray*

Special Delivery

"Who the hell is calling me at four in the morning?" I thought, as I reached over for the phone on the nightstand while glancing at the clock. I was dreaming that I was having a full body massage by a fine motherfucker, so I wasn't pleased at the interruption. "Hello?" I said groggily into the telephone receiver.

"Tasha, it's me Tammy, I've been looking for Worm for an hour with no luck, my water broke! Come please," I could hear the desperation in her voice and all the images of my full body massage disappeared.

"Ok I'm on my way!" I said and proceeded to get ready in a flash.

Tammy was moaning and squirming in my front seat as I rushed to Mercy Medical Center. She had a towel between her legs and as she held it tight, she yelled, "it's gonna come, it's gonna come, this baby is coming!" My adrenaline was at an all-time high, and as soon as I parked the car, I ran to retrieve a wheelchair and damn near picked Tammy up and put her in it. I pushed her into Labor and Delivery and we both were now yelling, "The baby is coming!" A slew of doctors appeared and took charge.

Tammy's contractions were coming closer and closer and sweat was dripping from her forehead as she attempted to deep breathe. I was calling around trying to locate Worm's ass which was more difficult than I had planned, as I realized I didn't know who the hell Worm had been rolling with nowadays. I got no answer from Mellie's phone so I left a voicemail on his long drawn out answering service just as Tammy yelled again, "Oooooch its happening!!" I sprinted to her side and wiped her face. Tammy was right! It was happening; I could see some curly hair between her legs. When the baby had descended far enough, the doctor asked Tammy if she wanted to feel the head, so she reached down to feel the head. That was when it really hit me that I was about to see a baby born. I felt all warm with excitement and I was ready to see the birth. Worm ran in, out of breath, just at that time and the nurse prepped him with a gown and head cover. He looked at me and mouthed, "Thanks big sis!" Then put on his mask.

Tammy eyes lit up and she let out a big scream. "Fuckkkkkk!!!" The doctor was telling her to slow down with pushing so she wouldn't tear, but Tammy pushed anyway and the head came out; it had one eye open ready to take a peek at

the world around. I saw her rip and she let out another scream, but it sounded more like a sigh of relief. Once the head was out, she gave two more decent pushes and the baby was into this world. They asked me to grab it, I tried, but it was slippery, and I saw he was a boy! They laid him on Tammy's chest and started drying him off to keep him warm. He didn't cry right away, but he was fine, still attached. He sneezed then he started to cry, a good healthy cry. He was so warm and squirmy and wet, but he was pretty clean. A little blood and some vernix. His head wasn't cone shaped, it was perfectly rounded. He wasn't red or wrinkled, his face wasn't squished. He was absolutely beautiful, and I regretted that abortion that I selfishly had done.

God works in mysterious ways, because on the same day Tammy delivered Ryan, later that evening our mother awakened from her coma. Everyone went over to the hospital but I only called. Worm told me that she was talking slowly and drinking fluids without difficulty. The doctors said she would fully recover with extensive physical therapy and she had asked if she could go straight to a Drug Treatment Inpatient Center. I didn't want to get my hopes up but I hoped Pam would really get her ass clean this time. I told Worm that I was physically exhausted but I laid in my bed wide awake until the sun came up. As I laid, I thought about the money and the two guns still in my possession, if Nate was being released soon, where was Rich if he wasn't dead and if he wasn't dead he was sure to be looking for me. I was in a fizzy! Nate really had me in a fucked up situation and as much as I should be mad at him, I missed him so much. I made a few calls and was finally given Nate's ID number, visiting hours and a strict dress code policy. As soon as 10am arrived, I was standing in line at Baltimore City Jail.

FML: FUCK MY LIFE
A novel by *Mimi Ray*

BCJ

It was chilly and although I had worn my black Triple Fat Goose, standing in the long line had my body numb. It was over twenty chicks standing in line in front of me. And one older man. There were young kids, too young for school, with snotty noses and dried tears on their faces. Most of the chicks were dressed in their finest, as if they were going to the club and I figured they didn't get the dress policy memo. I had on a pair of form fitting jeans, but not spandex material, and a red sweater with simple earrings and lip gloss. I felt that I looked appropriate for the situation but looking at the other chicks had me feeling like I was over dressed.

Finally it was my turn to register. They took my ID, frisked me, had me remove my shoes, belt and earrings and walked through the metal detector. Now I could understand why I had seen five chicks leave so fast, they weren't dressed accordingly or they didn't clear the detector. "Sucks to be them," I thought as I took a seat in the waiting area. There were a few inmates, with orange jumpsuits, cleaning the bathroom and mopping the floor. They were talking about robbery, homicide and rape nonchalantly as if they were eating lunch or something. I assumed they were low risk inmates, to be so close to the visitors. One by one, inmates

A novel by *Mimi Ray*

came out and took a seat behind a big black metal cage-like wall. I saw Nate walk in looking sexy as ever even in his orange jumpsuit, and sat down then the guard pointed to me, then pointed to the seat in front of him. I slowly approached him, and was unsure of what to say, so I just took a seat and he spoke, "what's up baby girl?" He smiled that million dollar smile and I felt warm all over. "Hi baby, how are you holding up? When are they letting you out?" I talked softly and he said, "you're gonna have to speak louder than that, with all these people talking. I'm not sure when the fuck I'm getting outta here. The bitch ass judge won't give me bail and I went up twice for review."

"Damn Nate," I spoke louder, "what am I going to do without you? I've been going through it. I feel lost and crazy. I miss you so much. How come you haven't called?"

"Calling isn't really an option, I come out for one hour a day, otherwise I'm in a cell, I shower and take care of business and if I'm lucky to get a free phone, I call Noel and check on things, it's really fucked up in here. My cell mate, don't wash his ass and I fucked him up twice and threw soapy water on him. I can't live like this but I don't want you to worry about me."

"I was so scared when you didn't show up at the hotel that---" I was saying before he cut me off.

A novel by *Mimi Ray*

"Let's not talk about that baby, but I heard that nigga skipped town. It's some dudes looking for him over some money he owed. So that's a lost cause for us."I felt sick, he just confirmed that Rich was alive, and I'm sure the money he spoke of was the $20,000 I had. I didn't know how to tell Nate but I thought that I should so I said, "The plan didn't work but I got something like 10 what should I do?" Nate's eyes brightened and he said "hold it for my lawyer. Damn girl you never cease to amaze me. I love you!" Just then the guard tapped my shoulder and I knew my time was up. "I love you too Nate!" I said and blew him a kiss.

"Well", I thought, "that wasn't so bad" as I walked to the waiting area to get my belongings from the small locker that I was assigned. The exiting process wasn't as long as the entrance process and as two women talked behind me I listened. One lady asked, "what's that smell?" and the other lady replied, "it's the smell of people." For me, it wasn't that detestable but it made the air very thick and heavy. I realized that my breathing was exerted. It was so stifling inside that once I got out, the air seemed very fresh even if I were right smack in the middle of a polluted city.

FML: FUCK MY LIFE
A novel by *Mimi Ray*

Ladies Night

My music was blasting with a new club mix tape and I was pumped about going out to a party with Zena. I couldn't even recall the last time I went out and shook my big ass but I was surely gonna make up for lost time. I knew I looked good after sliding into my new leopard print cat suit. I had finally made it to the mall yesterday and boy did I clean up! I spent $5,000 so fast, you would have thought it was my first shopping spree ever. I bought a pretty ass white gold & diamond tennis bracelet and the way it glistened against the light, I looked like a rich bitch ready for the world.

I told Zena that I would meet her at the address she gave me and after parking on the small dark street I double checked to be sure that I was at the right place. It was across from an old post office located behind Lexington Market and the club looked like a regular row house with a small sign "Club Bunns". "Never seen a club like this", I thought as I got out of my car after one final check in the mirror. My makeup was fierce and the red lipstick I chose to wear made me look like a hot whore, just the look I was going for! Shit after spending five stacks yesterday, saving ten stacks for Nate and caught up on my bills, I had about $1200 to my name. I knew I needed to find a new job and maybe next week I'll go searching, but tonight, these lips were sure to get me paid!

The club was small but comfortable, with a large dance floor to the left of the entrance and a long well stocked bar with two female bartenders and I had to give a compliment where compliments were due cause damn both of them was sexy as hell. I quickly glanced around and spotted Zena at the far end of the bar. She didn't see me as I walked up so I playfully went behind her and put my hands over her eyes. She laughed out loud and said "sexy ass Tasha, I know it's you," causing me to blush. We hugged and although we hadn't been intimate in a long time, she still made my pussy tingle.

Zena introduced me to a few of her friends and as I was enjoying my drink, a Tequila Sunrise, a nice looking brown skin guy with braids to the back, about 5'7 and dimples in each cheek sat down next to me. "What you drinking?" He asked me, and motioned for the bartender to come over. "Give her a refill," he said and the bartender did as he requested. I smiled and said, "Thank you," being sure to expose all of my perfect teeth. "No problem, sexy, I've never seen you here before," he said, and I realized his voice was rather soft. "Yea, it's my first time, it's pretty nice, laid back," I stated as I browsed the scenery. Just at that moment, I noticed he was the only guy in the whole club! Wait a minute? Was I drunk? I giggled and I said, "Looks

like your lucky night, you're the only guy in here!"
He leaned back, flashed a nice smile and said, "I'm
not a man, baby girl." I had a confused look on my
face and it must have been pretty evident, "Look
around sexy lady, it's a lesbian club." "Well I'll be
damned," I said out loud but basically to myself.
"Shocked huh?" The nice looking girl said. I looked
at her in a different light and still she was fine as
hell. "What's your name?" I inquired. "Toni, with an
I" she said."Nice to meet you, and thanks for the
drink," I said, extending my hand. She shook my
hands with a hand so soft and even though I knew
she was a woman, I was attracted to her. "She's a
sexy ass motherfucker," I thought to myself.
"Would you like to dance?" She asked. I laughed.
"I've never danced with a female before," I replied.
"It's easy as ABC, just like dancing with a man,
come on," and she grabbed my hand before I could
object.

I was having the time of my life dancing with
Toni, Zena and a few other chicks. We was
bumping and grinding each other as if it was a
natural occurrence for chicks to dirty dance
together. The more I danced the more turned on I
became and I couldn't understand why I was so
attracted to Toni knowing she was a girl looking
like a man. Even after all the encounters I had with
Zena, I still hadn't explored her body. It was always
her exploring me and me enjoying it. I was curious

about Toni and in my mind I laughed out loud, thinking "I bet she would eat some pussy up!!"

We danced, laughed and talked til closing time and as much fun as I was having I didn't want the night to end. Toni must have been thinking the same thing because she asked me would I like to go to Double T Diner and grab a bite to eat. I enthusiastically accepted. She asked was I okay to drive and after I said "sure", I saw her go over to one of her friends and say her goodbyes. As she walked I paid attention to her masculinity. She walked with a bop, her pants hung with her belt just below her waist, her braids reached the middle of her back and her ass was fitting her sweatpants very well. Damn she had it going on. I couldn't believe she was a chick, with all that swag.

Double T Diner was live. It was my first time there and although it was a restaurant, all the activity going on made it feel like a lounge. Toni ordered us both a drink, and I didn't mind. She had that dominating effect. She also suggested some of her favorite dishes, and I opted for shrimp stuffed with crabmeat and a side salad. I never was the type to be too cute to eat. Toni was

cool as shit. She seemed like a home girl I had known for years. Our conversation flowed and we didn't seem to pause at all. We had plenty to talk about. She was twenty-six, with no kids, worked as an accountant, owned a home and drove a Black

FML: FUCK MY LIFE
A novel by *Mimi Ray*

1993 Acura Legend. I was impressed. I wanted to ask her how did she become a lesbian but I didn't know how to ask. "It's been so nice talking with you tonight, I'm glad I took off work tomorrow," she said with a big smile. Her dimples were so deep they almost folded her cheeks in half. "I'm so glad we met, and I've equally enjoyed talking to you", I replied, lifted my glass, and said, "cheers to a new friendship", as we toasted.

I didn't know what these new feelings I were experiencing were but I constantly thought about Toni. Her demeanor, her aura, her style, just her. She was charismatic and she drew me in. I couldn't wait to see her again, next weekend, since she was working the rest of the week. She invited me to see a play, something I've never done and although I was excited for the play, I was super excited to see her. Even when I laid alone in my bed at night I would fantasize about Toni making love to me. I masturbated repeatedly and even moaned her name. Damn she had me lusting! Imagine what would happen if I managed to sleep with her! I was just about to step in the shower, after another self pleasure session when someone knocked on my door. "Who the hell is coming, uninvited?" I thought as I grabbed my robe and headed to the door. Out the peephole, I saw Pam standing there. The sight of her at my door caught me way off guard. I opened the door, wide and welcomed her in. She had never visited me at home, and I didn't even get the memo that she was out of the hospital. She came in and I offered her a seat and asked her if she wanted anything to drink, which she declined. "Listen Tasha, I didn't come here to make trouble. Every since I came out of that coma, I vowed that I would make my life right. I know I've never done right by you and the boys but I want to tell you, this time, unless God takes me from this earth, I'm making an oath to get my life together and all I'm asking for you is to have faith in me". I listened intently as she talked. She looked different. Her hair was growing out and she had it in a finger wave style. Her skin wasn't as dark and it appeared that she put on a few pounds. I began to speak, carefully selecting my words, "I'm not the one that you have to answer to. This is your life. Everyone is given a life and it's up to them to live their life to the best of their ability. The problem I have with you is that you chose to deliver four kids into this world. And you left us, with nothing, and unless this is your apology, you have yet to apologize. However, I forgive you. I'm almost eighteen, I'm grown, I survived this far and I plan to keep on keeping on." She said, "I appreciate it Tasha, I'm going to the twelve week rehab program tomorrow and once I'm complete, I'm trying to get Chink back. Thanks for talking with me, and I know you probably have doubts but I love you." I stood up, gave her a hug, and smiled.

After Pam left, I took a long hot shower. I let the water run all over my body as I washed my hair and I felt like I was cleansing my soul. It was refreshing. I said a prayer for Pam and my brothers. Praying wasn't something I was used to doing so I really didn't know what to say, but after saying, "Hello God, I know you know who I am. You've been watching me, I feel it, and I want to say thanks. As much as I've been going through I know it could be worst. Please take care of my mom and brothers and look out for Nate. Thank you", I felt that was sufficient. I stepped out of the shower and realized the phone was ringing. I ran for it but I missed the call. "Oh well, they'll call back", I thought, hopped in my bed and I drifted off to sleep.

FML: FUCK MY LIFE
A novel by *Mimi Ray*

1994

"I knew I was going to be late for work," I thought as I jumped up out of my cozy warm bed. It was my second day on my new job, administrative secretary, at Toni's office. She helped me tweak my documents to get hired. Although it was two weeks before my eighteenth birthday, the position required employees to be at least eighteen prior to starting. I was told after ninety days probation, I would get a raise but to be honest, I wasn't concerned with the money because I was just happy to be working so close to Toni. "Damn", I thought, rushing around putting my clothes on after just washing my face and brushing my teeth. "Where did the time go?" I didn't want to let Toni down. We had been hanging around each other for four months and I was on my best behavior. Even though I wanted to give her all of this pussy, she was reluctant to sleep with me. After learning that I had a boyfriend in jail and I was inexperienced with women, she explained that she didn't want her feelings hurt and thought it was best if we remained platonic friends. She was cool as shit so I didn't have a problem with that but I really couldn't deny the fact that I wanted her. I didn't even care that she was a chick. She turned me on entirely and although I was masturbating damn near every day, I yearned to be touched.

FML: FUCK MY LIFE
A novel by *Mimi Ray*

Pam was granted temporary custody of Chink and they had moved into a Section 8 apartment directly below Worm and Tammy. The last time I went over there, the kids were getting so big. Kashay was running around and every time she said "Auntie Tash" I cracked up. Baby Ryan was crawling around getting into everything and they both were so cute! It was such a joy being an aunt and I was proud of Worm for taking care of his family, even though he was still in the streets.

As I raced out of my apartment, hoping not to be too late for work, I checked the mailbox and it was a letter addressed to me from Booker. It wasn't the usual Victor Cullen address though and I was puzzled. I ripped open the letter, knowing I was going to be even later, but I had to read it right then.

Booker Thomas 1223445
Eastern Correctional Institution
30420 Revells Neck Rd., Westover, MD 21890
Dear Big Sis,

"By the time this letter reaches you, I hope it finds you in the best of health, physically, mentally and spiritually. I guess by now you've heard the news and if you haven't, seeing the new address tells you I've moved. They tryna charge me with first degree murder. Charging me as an adult. Ain't that a bitch. This dude ended up stabbed to death the day after we was fighting but believe me big sis, I didn't kill nobody. I hope everyone is good. I

heard Mommy is clean now. That's good. Maybe y'all can come see me. Send me some pictures and a money order please."
Love always, Booker

I felt so damn bad. I couldn't believe my little brother was in a real prison. Not boy's village. Not a jail. A real damn prison. He was still a fucking child unlike Nate. I didn't really worry too much about Nate's ass. I was sending him money orders weekly as he requested and visiting him once a month but things just didn't feel the same. Although I missed him dearly, the interest was falling off. And because he never wrote me back, I didn't know what the hell was really going on with him. His court date was approaching and I had purchased him some court clothes and sent him another package and he still hadn't fucking contacted me to say whether he received it or not. I was getting fed up with Nate's ass, and I wasn't sure if it was because I was falling for Toni or because of the lies and abuse I went through with him but I knew I was going to have to cut it off with him, depending on his outcome at court.

The next six hours at work, I thought about Booker. I called Worm to tell him about the letter and he wasn't surprised. Apparently he already knew, and so did Pam and Tammy. I was the last to know. I was beginning to feel like a fucking outsider and thought perhaps I needed to just start focusing on myself.

FML: FUCK MY LIFE
A novel by *Mimi Ray*

Turning Eighteen

The boss had told the truth when he said that I would get a raise after ninety days because it was day ninety-three, which fell on my birthday and when I opened my paycheck, I was thoroughly pleased. Damn Toni really hooked me up when she got me the job and I thought about what I could do to thank her. I was trying to get my mind off of Nate's court date which was two days away and I was still holding on to this $10,000 for his lawyer whom I was supposed to meet up with at the hearing. I called Toni's extension from my desk and waited for her to answer.

"Hey Toni", I said once she picked up, "what are you doing tonight? I know I said I didn't want to make a big fuss over my birthday, but my raise came through and I wanted to thank you. Maybe go out for a drink?"

"You know what, that sounds good, anything for the birthday girl!" she replied, sounding even more excited than me. I could hear her smile through the phone and my whole day felt happier. We agreed that she would pick me up at 8pm and head to Michael's in Timonium, MD as someone had recommended to me in the past. I didn't really care where we were going; I was eagerly waiting to just be around her sexy ass.

FML: FUCK MY LIFE
A novel by *Mimi Ray*

As soon as I got off work I headed straight to the hairdresser. I wanted to experiment and get some blonde streaks added to my long wrap. My burgundy color had faded a while ago and I was starting to look like a plain Jane. As I sat in the beautician chair I eavesdropped into chick's conversation. Most of them were talking about the same thing. The latest clothes and purses, the neighborhood drug dealers; who was getting paid and who was fucking who. It all seemed pretty boring to me since I hadn't been up to date on any of it. It made me recognize how I had changed because before, I could easily add to a conversation and I would know who the ballers were.

The chick who was doing my hair name was Mint and she was talking about every damn body. My ears perked up when she mentioned The City Jail. She was talking about her best friend, saying he was locked up and how long he had to wait for a court date. I could relate to her, thinking about Nate, but I didn't chime in.

"Girl I know all about that fucking city jail", a caramel complexion chick with big pretty light brown eyes said as she went to sit under the dryer. She was about 5'6 with a small waist and big bubble butt, reminding me of myself.

"My boo been down there for too damn long and my happy ass be faithfully in line every week to see my man!" she continued.

FML: FUCK MY LIFE
A novel by *Mimi Ray*

"I know that's right!" Mint exclaimed.

"He goes to court in two days and as long as this dumb broad he used to fuck with pays his lawyer, he'll be out in no time to fuck this tight pussy I've been saving!"

I instantly felt my temperature boiling. What kind of coincidence could it be that she was talking about Nate? But I didn't want to assume so I cut in. "Damn that's faithful, I know he's proud of you, what's his name?" I asked, looking into her eyes.

"Hell yea he's proud! His name is Nate!" She said like a happy school girl. I leaped from my chair and before anyone could comprehend what was happening I had my left hand holding her hand and my right hand punching her face. Over and over again. She was kicking and screaming.

"Bitch get the fuck out off me!" As she tried to get away. I slipped on some hair gel and fell backwards while still holding her hair. She tumbled on top on me. I managed to see my hand which was no longer in her hand but free, with a large clump of hair in it. I threw the hair and attempted to push her off of me. She punched me in my right eye. Fuck! That shit hurt. "Bitch you wanna fuck my man? Is that what you were saying?" I yelled as I made my way from under her. As soon as I was able to stand I grabbed her by the shirt and slung her to the floor. The chicks around us was cheering us on and I could hear Mint yelling "y'all bitches need to stop.

FML: FUCK MY LIFE
A novel by *Mimi Ray*

Y'all fucking shit up!! I'm calling the cops!!" At this point I didn't give a damn about any cops. I wanted her to know that fucking with Nate's cheating dirty dick ass was costing her an ass whopping. As she laid on the floor, I took one swift kick and said, "Bitch tell Nate to pay for his own fucking lawyer!" I grabbed my purse, handed Mint a $50 bill for my $35 hairdo and left the premises.

I was fucking heated. That low life pimple-faced bastard had tried to play me! I couldn't believe Nate had the audacity to have another chick, even in prison! I was livid! I wanted to get even and even was exactly what I planned to get.

It was 8pm sharp and I knew that the knock on the door was Toni. I wasn't ready. I was nowhere near ready. I didn't want her to see the scratches on my face and the dark ring around my right eye. I was embarrassed to even tell her that my eighteen year old, finally legal ass was fighting on my birthday. Dressed in dark blue boy shorts and a light blue tank top, I opened the door anyway.

"Hey sugar face", she said brightly, presenting me with a dozen of red roses.

"Awwww thank you so much!" I exclaimed hugging her and smiling. I backed away so she could come inside, and she immediately saw my black eye, ignoring my little shorts.

"Oh my God! Tasha what happened to you?" She asked with concern.

"It's nothing much, don't worry about it", I replied hoping she would skip the subject.

"How can you say nothing much? When I'm looking at a black eye?! Is that nigga out of jail? Did he do this to you?" she questioned as she raised her voice.

"No but I was fighting his girlfriend. Some chick at the hairdresser was talking shit about being his bitch and I went off", I explained. Toni went to my freezer, grabbed some ice and wrapped it in a hand towel. As she pressed it against my eye, she used her other hand to move my hair from my forehead.

"You're too pretty to be out there fighting, Tasha", she said in a soft tone. She was so close that the warmth of her breath made the tiny hairs in my nose tickle. Damn she turned me on. While she was tending to my eye, my perverted ass was already daydreaming that she would tend to my pussy. Yea she was that damn sexy. I felt myself tingling below.

"Well it's your birthday, and it's up to you if you still want to go out but I don't mind ordering in and staying here with you. The ball is in your court," she spoke still in that sexy soft tone of hers. "How about Chinese?" I asked, rather excited at the thought of staying in, alone, with Miss Sexy-as-she-wanna-be.

FML: FUCK MY LIFE
A novel by *Mimi Ray*

As we sat on the couch chit chatting waiting on our food delivery, I remembered I had a bottle of Cisco in the fridge. "Hey I got some Cisco, let me go grab it", I said while going into the kitchen before she declined. While pouring the drinks I could hear the knock on the door and I told her that the money was near the TV. She got the food from the delivery guy, sat it on the table and said, "Ok I'll be right back", and then it was silence. I set up my small dinette table; that I was glad I had purchased since I never got my dinette set from Nate's abandoned apartment. I briefly thought of Nate and in that same moment I thought "fuck that nigga!!" I prepared our dishes, shrimp lo mein for me, beef and broccoli for her. "Damn this smells good!" I said after hearing Toni return. She was carrying a large duffel bag. My curious mind wandered. "What you got there?" I asked inquisitively. "Ha ha ha, something you will love after you've had enough Cisco!" She said while laughing. I really wanted to know what was inside of her bag now.

I was definitely feeling tipsy after two glasses of berry Cisco and only a few bites of my food. We were talking and laughing so much that I hardly ate any of the delicious meal. I excused myself to use the bathroom, and while in there I freshened up. When I came back, I could see that Toni had set up her surprise. She had connected a karaoke machine up to my TV and handed me the microphone! I felt shy as hell! But I grabbed it and started singing, "Like a Virgin" laughing my ass off that she had chosen that song for me. We were still sipping and singing and when I glanced at the clock it was almost midnight. I didn't want the party to end but I was feeling tired and my damn eye kept thumping, reminding me of all of the days' events.

I remember walking Toni to the door, but everything that transpired afterwards was like a dream. We were in the doorway and as we hugged, our bodies connected and the next thing you know we were passionately kissing. She backed me into the apartment, shut the door and I was lying back on the couch. Still dressed in my boy shorts and tank top as she was slowly caressing me through my clothes. She was aggressively tender and I just laid back filled with lust and excitement. Slowly she kissed me on my neck and shoulders, her lips were so soft. She looked as if it was the moment she was waiting for, her beautiful eyes excited. So I leaned into her and slowly pressed my lips to hers, as I smirked. I felt her tongue move along my lower lip, asking for entrance. I opened my mouth, hers opening too, and her tongue plunged into my mouth, searching around to see what I had. I played with her tongue and locked my lips on hers, stealing some saliva from her mouth. This felt amazing. To be kissing my girl crush. I pulled her body closer to mine, still sucking on her tongue. I felt up her curvy

FML: FUCK MY LIFE
A novel by *Mimi Ray*

body as she pressed her chest to mine. God, I
wanted to undress her so so bad. But I had to take it
slowly with her, I didn't want to seem too eager.
Toni moved her hand to my breasts, putting her
hand under my shirt. She was reading my mind or
something. I was still sucking on her mouth, she
tasted delicious. Quickly I felt my tank top being
lifted off of me and over my head. I did the same to
her. I might as well if she was so eager, you know?
Our almost bare chests rubbed together. This was
the chance I had been waiting for. I took off her bra
to unveil her gorgeous massive breasts. Her nipples
were round and perky. She looked at mine and
pressed herself against me. Rubbing our nipples
together. It was goood.... I felt myself get hotter and
hotter. She was turning me on big time. She kept on
kissing me and started to rub between my legs. I
played with her nipples and made them get hard. I
moved my lips down her neck to her boobs and
started to suck on them, biting her nipples here and
there and rubbing hers hard. She was rubbing mine
hard too. She was a lot more confident than I
thought she would be. She stopped for a moment
and held my chin, looking me up and down. I was
sort of out of breath, and I smiled at her. She
smirked and kissed me again, while she took of my
boy shorts. I could feel myself getting hornier and
hornier. She stripped me, showing my pussy off and
my ass. She then stripped herself and we sat there

for a second, naked and both out of breath. Her body was just as sexy as I had imagined it be. She really hid those curves under her baggy clothes. As I stared at her, she pounced on me, kissing me and rubbing my clit with two fingers. I moaned and rubbed her tits and bit her nipples. She went faster and harder... My pussy started to produce sweet sweet juice. She moved down, her lips leaving a wet mark from my tits to my pussy. She started to lick... Begging for me to let her inside. I moaned and she giggled, licking my pussy and going right inside. I stopped her and winked. "Sixty... Niner..." I said, out of breath and begging her to let me lick her. Even though I never tasted pussy before, besides my own, I was eager to put my lips on hers. And as soon as I thought she was going to turn me down, she turned around, her fresh bald pussy perked at my face. I was drooling all over myself. My legs lay wide open for her and she started to rub me again, making me moan. So I started to suck on her pussy making her clench in surprise. I giggled and smacked her ass. "Tasty!" I said, as I started to rub her clit as I sucked on her pussy with my other hand, I rubbed my own boob and played with my nipple. We both went wild, sucking and poking and rubbing and biting. Toni went from fingering me with two fingers to almost fisting me... My pussy had never felt so good. My sweet juice poured all over the couch, making her and I both soaking wet.

FML: FUCK MY LIFE
A novel by *Mimi Ray*

I dove my tongue right into the depths of her pussy. She tasted so so so good. My first lesbian 69 and I loved it! Toni turned back around and started thrusting her pussy against mine. "Grinding?" I asked her, she nodded, too busy to talk. I moaned and let her experiment on me... I didn't mind at all. Thrusting harder and faster against me, I felt great. I moaned and thrust against her. It felt soooo good her big clit rubbing against my swollen clit! All of a sudden she let out a great yell and had a massive orgasm and when I felt her wetness blend with mine, I started to orgasm too.

FML: FUCK MY LIFE
A novel by *Mimi Ray*

Change of Plans

"You have a collect call from ....Nate", the computerized operator said after I answered the phone. "Why the fuck is he calling now?" I thought as I slammed the phone down. Just like a bitch ass nigga to call the day before court. I didn't feel like I had anything to say to him. The phone rang again and I knew it would be him calling back so I answered. "You have a collect call from...Nate." I pressed 1 to accept the charges.

"Hello?" I said nonchalantly

"Tasha don't play with me. What the hell is wrong with you girl?" Nate asked, annoying me instantly.

"It's not a damn thing wrong with me. Life is peaches and cream on my end. How may I help you?" I was trying to piss him off intentionally.

"Don't fucking play with me. I heard about your little stunt in the hair dresser yesterday. And I see you're on your best bullshit. I'm going to need you to take the money to the lawyer today", he said sharply.

"What money Nate? I thought your girlfriend was taking care of you and your lawyer business. At least that's what she said", I lied.

"Play with me if you want. Bitch don't ever forget who I am. You know what I'm capable of and if you don't want to be on my shit list I advise you to get the fucking money there by tonight", he threatened. But I wasn't scared.

"Fuck you, fuck your lawyer and fuck your time in jail! I hate you!" I yelled, tears forming in my eyes from a combination of hurt and anger. He had some effect on me but I was determined to fight it. I noticed he didn't reply.

"Hello?" I said into the phone. No reply. "Hello?" Still no reply.

Either Nate had hung up or the phone call time was up. I screamed, "fuckkkkkkkkk yoouuuuuuuuuu Nate!!" To no one but myself and slammed the phone down. The nerve of him to call. Plus he threatened me. Fuck him and his shit list. I promise I will not be at court tomorrow and I damn sure ain't going to

no lawyer tonight. My mind was made up. He hurt me enough. I no longer felt that he loved me. Unless he had a crazy way of showing it. I went into my bedroom and took out my writing pad.

Dear Booker,

"What's up baby bro? I know you're growing up but you'll always be my baby brother next to Chink. I was happy to hear from you but so sad to hear about the situation. I've been doing pretty good. Staying out of trouble and handling my

business. Life has a crazy way of showing us where our priorities should lie. I know I haven't been living up to my title as big sister, as I used to. I got side tracked and became selfish at some point and lost myself. Even now as I write, I'm not even sure who I am. I spent too long in an abusive relationship. Too long using my body and damaging myself. I never thought I would be all used up at 18 years old but here I am, just living. I know things could always be worst, and I'm not complaining. I just wish I could turn back the hands of time. Things would be so different. I'm going to do my best to stay in touch with you.

    But if I fall off track, keep this lawyer information.

    Atty Lenny Hunt
    1122 East Chase Street
    Baltimore, Md 21213
    410-555-1222

    I'm giving him money to take care of you. We will get you out of this. Inside is a money order for $100 and two pictures. I'll take more pictures soon. I'm usually too tipsy by the time the picture man shows up. :)

    Love you eternally,
    Big Sis

I folded the letter, signed the money order, placed them together with the pictures, licked the stamp and sealed the envelope. I called the lawyer, thankful that I had saved that business card from one of the clients at work. Even if Booker wasn't cleared, at least I knew with $10,000 he would have a lawyer to fight for him. As for Nate, "good luck", I thought and made my way to the post office.

FML: FUCK MY LIFE
A novel by *Mimi Ray*

Christmas

It didn't feel like Christmas but the music that played in the office all month reminded everyone that it was the season to be jolly. I was hella surprised last week when Pam called to say she was having Christmas dinner at her place and that no one needed to bring anything but themselves. Since I played house with Toni over our whole Thanksgiving vacation, I knew I better spend Christmas with the family. When it came to Christmas, what more can I say…Of course it is the most beloved holiday of the year, a celebration of hope, understanding, sharing and the list remains open. But for me, I could give a damn about celebrating Christmas. For me, it reminded me of the freezing cold winter months we dreaded, growing up. When we had illegal gas and electric, it didn't include free heat. I used to turn the oven on and light all four burners on the stove to heat the house. Since it only heated the first level, we would take all of the blankets that we had and sleep on the cold ass dining room floor, closest to the kitchen. Christmas, as we grew up it was nothing special. Pam ass was never around and I can only remember one damn gift, a rabbit; that was shared between Worm and I. We fought over the rabbit for two days and on the third day the rabbit was gone. I knew

FML: FUCK MY LIFE
A novel by *Mimi Ray*

Pam had got rid of it because she didn't like all of that noise. When she would come in from her overnight escapades, we was told to sit at the foot of her bed, shut the hell up and watch television until it was time to go outside and play. I hated the winter for various reasons and most of all, I hated the snow. When I was about nine years old, it was a blizzard. Instead of Pam checking the news to see of schools was closed, she just sent us out in the snow. The snow was up to my chest, and poor Worm, it was up to his neck. We walked across the half mile long field, and up the road, creating a path so deep it was like a tunnel. We finally reached school, a usual fifteen minute walk, after an hour walk in the snow. And the fucking school was closed. The principal answered the door for us, called Pam to tell her that school was closed because of the blizzard, and Pam trifling ass said, "oh well send them back!" Across the field we went and after three hours of thawing out, I could finally feel my limbs again but the frostbite lasted for days. Yes I hated winter, but I had a niece and a nephew now, so I'll grin and bear it and go to Pam's for Christmas.

Everyone seemed to be having a good time when I arrived. I took my sweet time coming, just so I wouldn't be the first one there. Kashay and Ryan had so many toys opened, it looked like they lived there instead of upstairs. Chink was playing a video game and Tammy was helping Pam in the kitchen. I had to admit, the food was smelling good and I realized I hadn't had an home cooked meal since Zena fixed it. I made a mental note to take a plate home for Zena, since she had told me she was working tonight. Toni was with her family so I really had no reason not to be with mine. "Where's Worm?" I asked Tammy after I came back from my trance. "He said he will be here by 5:30, you know him, always business", she answered, as she was stirring cornbread mix. Tammy, Pam and I made small talk and I noticed we didn't have much to talk about. I told them I had hired a lawyer for Booker and that I had met with him three times over the last three months. I talked about how the state was gathering evidence and he was making talk about DNA which was the new talk of town. I told them that I heard that Nate's court date was postponed for a year and that something came up and he was moved to the federal jail. Pam asked me was I dating anyone and I lied and said no. I guess I wasn't ready to tell the family that I was a lesbian. I wasn't even sure if I was a lesbian since I still thought about dick sometimes when I masturbated. I probably was bisexual but I would have to fuck a guy to be sure, and since it had been so long since I had, I just assumed I was gay. Anyway, I lied. I was dating Toni, my boo, who treated me better than any man. Well she treated me just as good as

FML: FUCK MY LIFE
A novel by *Mimi Ray*

Scooter. I missed Scooter. I couldn't figure out why my mind wouldn't stay on track. It seemed to jump from subject to subject and I couldn't focus on Christmas at all. I was actually relieved when Worm arrived, so I could talk to him instead of Pam and Tammy but Worm stayed on his phone. I even remarked, "it's Christmas boy, put it on hold til tomorrow". He just laughed, and made call after call. I was sooooo ready to go and when it was time to eat, I gobbled my food down, skipped dessert and hugged everyone before they could realize I was leaving. I was out of there so fast, that I even forgot to make a damn plate for Zena!

Once I got home, I saw I had three missed calls. I was appreciative that Toni had given me a Caller ID for an early Christmas gift. One call was from Zena, the other from Toni, then it was two numbers that I didn't recognize. I checked my answering machine. "Hello Tasha, I just wanted to say Merry Christmas. May you continue to be blessed, call me later". That was Zena. "Hey baby, I know you're at your moms just sending you some love, I'll call you tomorrow". Toni's voice had me blushing. The next voice was unexpected. "Yea I'm still around. Out of sight out of mind as the saying goes. I heard your freak ass out there eating pussy now. You are one trifling ass whore. Don't forget that I made you and just as easy as I made you, I can easily break you down. Oh yea Merry

FML: FUCK MY LIFE
A novel by *Mimi Ray*

Christmas, you HOE! HOE! HOE!" Nate said with
a chuckle in his voice. "Why couldn't he just leave
me alone??" I thought, as I went to double check
my locks and pull my blinds down. "Maybe it's time
to move", I thought as I got undressed. His message
had me tossing and turning all night.

FML: FUCK MY LIFE
A novel by *Mimi Ray*

It's Legal

The whole week following Nate's calls, I had nightmares. So many different kind of nightmares. From being chased by bees and stung to death and being drugged by a car until all of my limbs were ripped off to being eaten by a giant lizard. I was feeling worn down and tired and I decided at the beginning of the year, I would move from Scooters apartment. My mind was playing tricks on me and I even started thinking that I was seeing spirits. Not the actual ghost, since I wasn't sure if I believed in ghosts, but drifts of clear spirit like figures floating around the apartment. Maybe Scooter was ready for me to go and after I thought of everything that transpired since his death, I felt it was time to go.

Living an honest life and working 9 to 5 only seemed to pay the bills. I was starting to yearn for extra cash and as much as I didn't want to revert to my old ways, I knew how easy it was to make quick money. I met a variety of people working at the accounting firm, and one particular client stood out. I was assisting her with her taxes when she used a code 99999, and listed her job as "other". When I asked her what kind of work she did, she said "legal prostitution". Although we both laughed at her answer, I started to search the Internet and I actually found two escort services in the Baltimore region. I looked in her file, called her, told her I was looking for work and she connected me with her boss.

Reaching the boss was no problem. He asked a few interview like questions. Told me what was expected of me and of the clients. Gave me an overview of how the interview process would go and set me up for the very next night. He was located in Glen Burnie, Md and when I got to the address I pressed the intercom to be buzzed in. It was a large condominium, nicely decorated and the doors opened automatically. The Boss introduced himself but he didn't shake my hand which made me feel nervous. Although, I could tell from his voice over the phone, that he was a white man, I never thought he would be handsome. He was tall, at least 6 feet and his body was toned and muscular. He had silky black hair, hazel eyes, and a cleft in his chin.

The television was on and he was just finishing up his dessert of some sort. He asked me if I wanted anything but I declined. After a few phone calls he had to make, we started the photo shoot as he said it was needed in order for me to book clients. I never had a photo shoot before, but it was basically as I expected, except sexier. We used two outfits that I was told to bring, a skin tight black leotard and purple halter dress. Then I posed topless, with only a black and red lace thong on. Another outfit I chose was one he had for the girls, which was a black and white school girl skirt and a sheer white body shirt. I posed topless with just the skirt on as well. After that, we got down to business. He took a quick shower and then led me to the bedroom, where I started off massaging his back. Then we switched and he massaged my back. As the massage went on, it was starting to be clear that he had a foot fetish. He had me rub my soft smooth feet on his dick, which was growing harder. He was also alternating that with sucking on my toes, which no one had ever done, so that was interesting but I really didn't like it. Soon he had me flipped over, and he started to eat my pussy. Nothing special but I gave him some obligatory moans; my mind was strictly in business mode. Then he started rubbing on my nipples, asked me if my nipples were sensitive and I told him they were. I rubbed his dick with my hand for a little bit and that was the first time I noticed the actual size of it. It wasn't too long, average length, but its girth was enormous. I was a little worried since I hadn't been penetrated by anything other than Toni's toys in so long. But after he put on his condom, lubed himself up, he eased it in with swiftness. I wasn't really focused on anything besides getting it over and getting my money but once I realized he could fuck, my pussy started liking it. He was long-winded too. Maybe it's because he owns an escort business, who knows. But he even stated many guys can't stand up to a fraction of his stamina and apparently he can't cum from sex. The whole time he was showering praise after praise about me. But it was quite a workout, and I was thinking that I probably was going to lose weight from this job. I held up a pretty long time riding his thick white dick before I was just too tired. He then stroked himself until he busted off, squirted on my stomach while looking at my "pretty black butterfly", as he called it. I asked him how my audition went, and he laughed and said A+. I got $500 and he said I didn't have to give him the usual thirty percent cut from my first client, once it was booked. I was excited as hell. A new job!

FML: FUCK MY LIFE
A novel by *Mimi Ray*

New Years

"I've really out done myself this time", I thought, as I looked over my outfit in my full length mirror. The red Patton Leather Prada dress was worth the money I spent. It accented my every curve and my ass looked like it had been sculpted to perfection. Thankful to the squats Toni showed me how to do, I was standing like a stallion. My silver glitter peep toe shoes and silver clutch set it off with my favorite tennis bracelet and solitaire diamond necklace that draped my neck. And I was flaunting my long individual braids that hung down to my ass. It was New Years Eve and I was more than excited to be celebrating with Zena and Toni at some lavish party that Zena had tickets to. I didn't even ask if it was a lesbian affair, and I guess it didn't matter cause I was amped about shaking my ass.

The party was definitely not a lesbian affair. The sexy ass niggas that flooded the floors, looked like they had traveled from out of state or either the Baltimore dudes was really outdoing themselves tonight. It was ballers all through the three story mansion and from the reaction on others chicks faces, it must was some local celebrities in the place as well. I was pleased that I had chosen my attire. I didn't see any look a likes and even if I was to come across one, I know for damn sure she couldn't have rocked it like me. I was displaying my diva status persona and turning heads with every step I took. Zena and Toni looked sexy as well, but I had to admit I was the shit tonight. I started with my usual light wine, I had grown to adore since dating Toni and took a seat on one of the many plush couches that were decorating the shiny marble floor.

I saw him from across the room. My eyes, which had been merely scanning everyone, caught on to him and couldn't move. The comfort and ease with which he seemed to own the room, I could tell it wasn't his first time here. My mind raced at a lightning speed. I never thought I would see Rich alive, standing there, breathing and moving around like nothing never happened. I watched him throw his head back in laughter, so carefree. For so long, I hadn't thought about Rich. When Nate said he skipped town, I just thought of that as vanishing. I never thought he would come back. And not only come back but be in the same room where I was. I kept looking in his direction. I was positive it was him. Then his eyes slowly slid to meet mine. Every thought escaped me as I stood frozen by the intensity of his stare. A smile curled his full lips. I wondered if he recognized me then became mad at myself for allowing him to even see me. I tilted my eyes to the floor and turned my back to him, hiding my face. I needed to find Toni and Zena and get the fuck out of there fast!

I nearly jumped out of my damn skin when I felt a hand on my arm. I turned, afraid of the unknown, and it was him! His beautiful brown eyes were the exact same way that I remembered, before I thought that he died. I just wanted to say I was so fucking sorry and offer to pay my debt with unlimited sex on demand. But he just smiled at me, flashing a gorgeous smile and began introducing himself as if he didn't eat the hell out of my pussy! What the fuck!!!

FML: FUCK MY LIFE
A novel by *Mimi Ray*

About The Author

Mimi Ray, spent a few of her childhood years on a farm in New Jersey. During her elementary years, she moved back to her place of birth, Baltimore, Maryland and life was never the same.

Receiving her education in Baltimore City Public Schools, Mimi didn't feel challenged so she dropped out at age 14, pursuing her GED and obtaining her first AA degree in Accounting at age 18. Currently she works as a Licensed Practical Nurse, passionately spreading her care to everyone who comes into contact with her.

She accredits her big smile to her daughter Goddess, age 5, her son Da'God, age 14 and her supportive encouraging husband Shawn. Mimi enjoys reading, writing and hanging out with friends.

FML: FUCK MY LIFE
A novel by *Mimi Ray*

FML: FUCK MY LIFE
A novel by *Mimi Ray*

Connect with Mimi Ray on facebook @
Authoress Mimi Ray

Made in the USA
Charleston, SC
26 January 2014